BLOOD OF THE BOAR

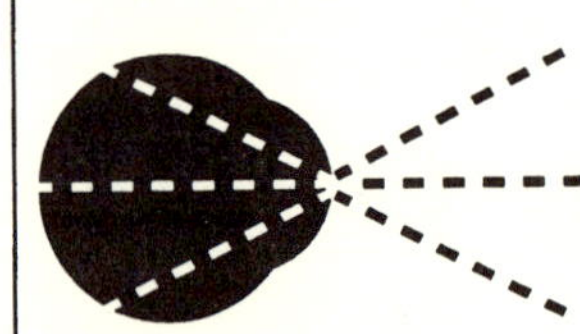
This Large Print Book carries the
Seal of Approval of N.A.V.H.

BLOOD OF THE BOAR

Margaret Abbey

Thorndike Press • Thorndike, Maine

Thorndike Large Print ® Romance Series edition published in 1993 by arrangement with Margaret York.

The tree indicium is a trademark of Thorndike Press.

Set in 16 pt. News Plantin by Ginny Beaulieu.

This book is printed on acid-free, high opacity paper. ∞

Library of Congress Cataloging in Publication Data

Abbey, Margaret.
    Blood of the boar / Margaret Abbey.
        p. cm.
    ISBN 1-56054-617-4 (alk. paper : lg. print)
    1. Large type books. I. Title.
[PR6051.B28B58   1993]
823'.914—dc20
                                                            93-13142
                                                               CIP

Dedication
For Doris Adams
in gratitude for
all her help and
advice over the
years.

<table>
<tr><td colspan="6" style="text-align:center">EAST GRID STAMP</td></tr>
<tr><td>BB</td><td></td><td>SS</td><td></td><td>MM</td><td></td></tr>
<tr><td>BA</td><td></td><td>SB</td><td></td><td>MW</td><td></td></tr>
<tr><td>BT</td><td></td><td>SC</td><td></td><td>MC</td><td>3/96</td></tr>
<tr><td>BR</td><td></td><td>SD</td><td></td><td>MD</td><td>3/95</td></tr>
<tr><td>BY</td><td></td><td>SE</td><td></td><td>MO</td><td>4/03</td></tr>
<tr><td>BC</td><td></td><td>SW</td><td></td><td>MY</td><td></td></tr>
<tr><td>BG</td><td></td><td>SL</td><td></td><td></td><td></td></tr>
<tr><td>BH</td><td></td><td>SV</td><td></td><td></td><td></td></tr>
<tr><td>BS</td><td></td><td></td><td></td><td></td><td></td></tr>
<tr><td>BN</td><td></td><td></td><td></td><td></td><td></td></tr>
</table>

One

May 1, 1484

"Mistress, go with the master and the children. The boy is deep off and will not stir. If he does, Luce will feed him right away. She's a good girl. You know she is."

Catherine looked fondly down at her sleeping son. As Margery said his eyes were closed fast and a little dribble of milk oozed contentedly from his pursed, rose-petal mouth. The redness and crumpled ugliness of birth had already deserted him and he was a beautiful child of whom Hugh could be justly proud. He was almost six weeks old, born with a minimum of discomfort, considering the difficulties and perils which had assailed his mother during the early months following his conception. She recalled, with an inner shudder, the horrors of October last, when Sir Hugh Kingsford had been imprisoned at Warwick Castle on suspicion of treason during the abortive rising of the Duke of Buckingham. Henry Stafford had paid for his folly on a hastily erected scaffold in Salisbury market place last November, when his head had been struck from his body. Hugh had been more fortunate.

The King had listened to her pleading when she had ridden desperately with Rob Wentworth from Warwick to Leicester. She had known then, in October, that their fierce coupling on the night following the coronation, would bear fruit. Hugh's first son — outside she could hear six-year-old Richard's tones, shrill with excitement. All here at Kingsford believed her elder child Hugh's son and her husband was content that it should be accepted so. The secret she had confided to the King in her anguish must remain safe-held between the three of them, yet Hugh had been so overcome with joy when she had placed the baby in his arms. He promised to be dark like his father, as Richard was, too, praise the Virgin, so none would guess —

Hugh had smiled down at her, anxiety causing that scar which winged his right brow, the result of an arrow graze at Barnet, to seem oddly sinister.

"The saints be praised you are safe, dear heart."

"He is small but healthy, Hugh, the midwife tells me. God has been good."

He had stooped to kiss her, the swaddled

babe held awkwardly but tenderly still in his arms.

"We will name him Hugh," she had whispered, reaching up to touch the crisp, dark curl which had fallen onto his brow. Already Hugh was greying and he only this last month thirty-two. Gloucester had said when their marriage had been suggested and she had cried despairingly that the man was old, "He is twenty-six, some seven months older than I am."

"I would have him named Wilfred, for your father," he said and her tears fell then onto the linen sheet. They were half of sadness, half delight that he had wished it. Sir Hugh had received her father's manor of Newburgh near Gloucester, following Sir Wilfred's execution and attainder at Tewkesbury. It had been partly to grant her some share of that inheritance that Gloucester had arranged her marriage to Sir Hugh Kingsford of Cadeby in Leicestershire over seven years ago at Middleham. So her second son had been baptized Wilfred Hugh in the parish church here in Cadeby by Father John.

Now it was May Day. Cecily and Janet, Hugh's daughters by his first wife, Ellen, who had died at Janet's birth, young Richard and Tom Walters, the steward's son, were all clamouring to go down to the village for the celebrations. Cecily was home from the convent at Tewkesbury where Catherine had taken her last October. She had been with them briefly over the Holy Season of Christmas, but Mother Superior had dispatched her two months ago to be with her family once more during the period of her step-mother's lying-in. Hugh was already in the courtyard attempting to quell Richard's impatience.

Margery sat near the cradle, her foot on the rocker, nodding reassurance.

"The sun is pleasant. You need the change. Go now, my lady. This is a true day for rejoicing for us all."

Catherine went to her bedchamber for a cloak, for it was still chilly in the wind. Cecily's light shoes pattered up the stair and she came to her step-mother's side.

"The new gown really becomes you."

Catherine glanced at her image in the small mirror of fine Venetian glass which had been one of Hugh's extravagant wedding gifts. He had insisted on the purchase of this new green velvet when the pedlar had come to the manor at Easter from Leicester.

"For when your figure returns to normal, my lovely Catherine," he had whispered, kissing her throat, as her fingers moved caressingly over the softness of the material. Her heavy fair hair had been loosened then, her movements ungainly, now the veiling newly stiffened on her fashionable butterfly hennin hid the golden mane from sight and the soft leathern belt with its gilded studs set off to perfection the returned litheness of her form.

Cecily followed her gaze and she touched the gown fleetingly.

"Green for the Maying. Mother Superior would frown on our heathen customs, but my father will welcome the sight of you, just as you are now. You really are beautifully recovered, Catherine. Each day my prayers to the Virgin are full of gratitude."

There was a special bond of affection between Catherine and her step-daughter and she drew the girl close to kiss her forehead.

"I think our rites are harmless enough. The children enjoyed so much going with Martine last night to bring in the May boughs. You did yourself, Cecily, other years, I'm sure."

"Indeed, I did."

The two women hastened down the stair to be greeted by the rest of the family with cries of delight. Richard jumped up and down excitedly, unable to contain himself.

"*Mamon,* you are quite beautiful. Like an angel, is she not my father?" He always addressed her in the French fashion since the early days following his birth they had spent at the Burgundian Court of the Duchess Margaret, the King's sister.

"More like some pagan huntress goddess, perhaps," Hugh said smilingly, "but every bit as beautiful. Now we are all assembled at last, let us be off to the village or I swear Richard and Tom, here, will run off without us."

It was only a short step on foot to the small green near the west door of the church. The children scampered ahead with Janet in hot pursuit. Cecily held back for a moment or two, feeling such hoydenish behaviour no longer in keeping with her professed desire to enter the noviciate next year, then, drawn by the spell of the pipe and tabor she could hear ahead and her younger sister's exhortations to "Hurry, please, Cecily, we shall miss the choosing of the May Queen," she threw caution to the winds, lifted her skirts and ran after the others.

Hugh put out his hand to take Catherine's.

"We have come safely through the storms, my wife, and now summer is ahead."

She nodded as his hand squeezed hers tightly and gave a little joyful breath. The trees were green again, the white mayflower in bloom, everything springing towards fulfilment.

Father John greeted them respectfully.

"Sir Hugh, my lady. Will you do us the honour, sir, of crowning our May Queen?"

Hugh smilingly acquiesced. The innkeeper's daughter, Meg, a pretty buxom fifteen-year-old, sat on a stool on the green, her attendants and swains about her. Her thick, brown hair fell loose onto her white robe. Today she seemed to be the one maid not clad in the traditional May-Day green. Hugh kissed her rosy cheek and stooped to adjust her crown of flowers and may blossom. Catherine gave her an embroidered ribbon as a keepsake. The villagers cheered and the Jack-in-the-Green capered forward, followed closely by the comic knight on his hobby horse.

Catherine's eyes followed the rector's to the capering Green Man.

"Are the rites truly pagan, Father?"

"They are. I fear, daughter," he acknowledged ruefully, "Buried deep in the lore of a people who worshipped Mother Earth and practised fertility customs." He shrugged. "I cannot find it in my heart to forbid my parishioners their joy in this day. They work so hard and the saints know their happiness and very survival depend on whether the earth is fruitful and the weather propitious."

Catherine frowned as she watched the fantastic, bush-covered dancer weave his way in and out of the crowd, Richard and Tom, cavorting in pursuit with the rest of the village children. She was vaguely repelled by the sight, remembering some reference long ago in childhood, perhaps, by her old nurse, Anna, to the old days when the gods required a living sacrifice for the corn to grow tall and green in the fields till it turned golden under the hot suns of July and August.

She turned, smiling, to Hugh as he joined her again at the commencement of the dancing round the garlanded Maypole tree. Soon the ale was flowing and the dancers becoming wilder in their gyrations. Hugh called the children to him and they took their leave of Father John and prepared to return to the manor house.

"*Mamon*, the fun will go on for hours yet," Richard objected.

"Nevertheless, young man, it is time for you to prepare for your bed," Hugh said firmly. "I know you boys. Now the nights get longer you will want to be off fishing and trapping hares when your lessons with Father John are over for the day. It will be an exhausting summer, my lad, and you'll need your sleep."

Janet was still panting with the exertion of the dance. She turned back a little curiously as Rob Wentworth, their groom, ran from the green with his arms flung possessively round a woman whose brassily golden hair had slipped free from her wimple and stirred a chord in Catherine's memory. Maud Daly!

The woman had taken her place that terrible day last October when she'd been kept a prisoner in her own house under the watchful gaze of the King's captain, Jehan Trêves. By Maud's action she had fled to Kineton to warn Hugh of his peril. Her eyes misted. She wished Maud well and Rob, too, dear, faithful Rob!

Someone called to Hugh urgently and he signalled to his steward, Jem Walters.

"Escort my lady to the house, Jem. It seems I am needed."

"Indeed, Sir Hugh."

Alice, Jem's wife, did not seem sorry to leave the festivities now becoming openly boisterous and amorous.

"I'm thankful, my lady, I'm sure, to be going home to my own fireside. My new shoes are pinching me cruelly."

It was when they entered the front courtyard that Catherine saw the grooms leading away the strange horses.

"A visitor." Richard crowed with delight at yet another chance to possibly delay his bedtime.

"It seems so," Catherine turned to Alice Walters. "Please see that Richard with Tom is fed, Alice."

Her heart turned over and she clung to the door post as her visitor turned from the fire burning brightly in the hall for the stone struck chill despite the May sun outside.

"Monsieur Chauvet."

He bowed with that courtly extravagance she had always felt faintly mocking. Nothing could dispel one's little gasp of astonishment at first sight of that remarkable personal beauty. He had pulled off his velvet cap and those reddish brown curls were as well tended and cut as his fine dark doublet and hose. The cloak he was now removing bore the stains of the mud and dust of early summer acquired on an obviously urgent ride. She caught the glint of those cold green eyes of his as he bent to kiss her hand in greeting.

"Madame Catherine, I rejoice to see you so well."

"Our steward and bailiff are at the May ceremonies, Hugh with them still. Please sit, near the fire, sir, while I dispatch a serving wench for refreshment."

A girl came at her call.

"Mulled ale, and malmsey." She turned to her visitor. "You will dine with us, stay the night?"

"If Sir Hugh permits."

"He will welcome you, sir, as I do."

The girl's feet pattered off down the corridor and Catherine moved closer to him. She felt strangely unwilling to discover the cause of his errand. The day had been so blissful and Chauvet's arrival had blotted the halcyon blueness of sky with a darkening cloud of unease. She found herself murmuring housewifely phrases she knew to be inane, as if she would put off the moment of truth.

"You ride from the Court, Monsieur Chauvet?"

"Yes, from Nottingham. I bear a christening gift from His Grace for your little son, and the Queen's letter of congratulation."

Catherine felt a warm flush of relief mounting to her throat and cheeks. So that was it. Richard had found time to remember the welfare of his previous ward and graciously send word of his pleasure at the safe birth of her son. Her presentiment of doom at sight of the Burgundian had been foolish. Hugh would say, later, that her condition, so soon following her delivery, had rendered her prone to such forebodings.

"Their Graces are very kind. Little Wilfred is a strong boy. We are overjoyed. You must see him, Monsieur Chauvet, and report back to the Queen. Is she well — and the King's Grace?" She could never be sure if she betrayed herself whenever she spoke of him and was grateful that Hugh was not present to hear her first, anxious enquiry. This strangely perceptive man appeared to have the ability to read her innermost heart. He had always had this disturbing effect on her peace of mind, from the night he had driven out the midwife who stank on that dreadful day at 'The Crossed Keys' in London when she had lost Hugh's first child over a year ago. Perron Chauvet had saved her life. She smiled inwardly as she recalled how condescending Hugh had then been to the man he considered merely a barber surgeon and then discovered him to be the second son of a Burgundian count and a messenger between the Protector's household and the Court of Margaret of Burgundy. That Chauvet should be interested in surgery and had studied under the Moors and Saracens had been puzzling enough, but that he should have the ear of the Protector, now King Richard, was odder still and she had wondered, long and deeply, about the reason for Richard's undoubted and surprising trust in this man.

"I had hoped to be with you — in time but I was kept at Middleham."

There was no mistaking his meaning and she coloured. Chauvet's concern for her last year, in London, had aroused Hugh's fury, now the Burgundian made it plain that his interest had not lessened, then the second part of his answer hit her with full force. Her eyes widened in returned alarm.

"Middleham? The Prince —"

"Is dead, Madame Catherine." He shook his head gently as she gave a little heart-broken cry. "I regret there was no way I could soften the blow for you. I know you had true affection for the Prince of Wales. The Queen explained and I myself have heard him speak of you."

"Oh, no. Dear God, the Queen! How — how can she bear it? I-I —"

"When did this happen, Monsieur Chauvet?"

Hugh came in and drew close to her chair. She reached blindly for his hand as she attempted to check her tears.

She had last seen the boy at Middleham, over seven years ago, a bright, forward, friendly child, eager to show his prowess on his first pony. She could not bear to think of his parents' anguish. Hugh's hand tightened on hers in comfort.

"April the ninth. I rode immediately to Nottingham to inform His Grace. He and the Queen had only recently set up Court there after leaving Cambridge."

"What — what was wrong?"

"He had ailed throughout the winter. I had been sent with several of the King's household to deliver messages and report back to His Grace."

Catherine could well believe that Richard,

knowing the man to be knowledgeable in surgery and medicine, might easily have considered Chauvet as highly suitable to send on such
an errand not realizing —

"The Prince took a chill which settled on
his chest. He has always been delicate, I understand, and seemed not to have the strength
to fight it. There was nothing we could do.
He died early in the morning, having received
the last rites. He did not suffer greatly, Madame Catherine. Give your so tender heart
peace. It was so sudden Dr Hobbes had not
time to send advance warning of the illness
to the King."

"How have they taken it?" Her voice was
little more than a pain-filled whisper.

"Badly, of course. The poor Queen is quite
distracted, *la pauvre petite,* and taken to her
bed. His Grace —" Chauvet shrugged expressively, "you know the King, *naturellement.* He
bears the blow with fortitude, keeps up a so
brave front both for her sake and for his courtiers, but —"

"This is a body blow to his kingship and
power as well as his natural distress as a loving
father," Hugh said heavily.

Chauvet spread his hands once more in that
Gallic gesture Catherine knew well. The maid
approached and stood, nervously aware of the
dire nature of the visitor's tidings, and unsure

whether she should enter the hall.

"Come in, Agnes. Serve Monsieur Chauvet and ask that accommodation be made ready for him to-night and see his groom be fittingly bestowed."

"Yes, Sir Hugh." She sketched a hurried curtsey and put down the tray. As she reached the doorway Hugh recalled her.

"Ask Margery to see that Richard is put to bed and request that my daughters join us at supper."

"The King and Queen will travel North at once?" Catherine asked. "Will they bury the Prince in Westminster?"

"Nothing had been decided when I left. The Queen requested that I ride to you — with the news. She had been so delighted to hear that you — she loves you well, Madame Catherine."

"The Virgin knows how I do her. She took pity, long ago, on a child ruined by the late Wars —"

Catherine broke down and wept. The two men watched, soberly, neither attempting to prevent her, both tacitly agreeing that her grief needed to be given full rein.

She lay wakeful that night, staring upwards to the high roof timbers. Mentally she reviewed the happy hours she had spent in the company of the young Prince. She had been with him that day when Gloucester had offered her a white, Yorkist rose and she had refused to take it from his hand. A great shudder went through her frame. She had cursed him and all his house for the harm they had done her and then, in the wood, where he found her after she had fled from him, she had known how she loved him and he had ridden home to Middleham holding her close to his heart lest she further injure her arm after Lovell's horse had thrown her.

How could he bear this terrible loss of his son and heir? And Anne, his Queen, unable to give him another child. Only last year Catherine had anxiously watched the Queen, knowing the deadly signs of lung sickness, she had learned to recognize during her stay at the convent in Tewkesbury where she had often assisted the infirmarian, the bouts of coughing, the hectic flush on the cheek bones and the traces of blood on her kerchief that the Queen was at pains to keep hidden from her husband.

And now another terror had Catherine in its grip. Had Perron Chauvet come here only on his declared errand, Richard —

Hugh stirred at her side.

"Can you not sleep?"

She turned to him instinctively. He was very tender with her. Hugh always treated her with the utmost consideration, tempering his desires with restraint. He knew well she had not yet fully recovered from the birth of little Wilfred. As always, at such moments, she was consumed with the bitterness of guilt. She loved Hugh, had deep respect for him, but always her longing to be within the King's sight gnawed at her conscience. She knew well enough that knowledge haunted Hugh's peace. Now, banished here to his own estates, he must have hour upon hour to dwell upon the hard reality of his wife's love for another.

Yet he loved Richard too — dearly.

His hand gently stroked her hair.

"Try not to grieve too deeply, dear heart."

"What can he do? At least while the succession was sure there was a measure of hope for the peace of the realm. Now, whom will he choose?"

"His sister's son, young John of Lincoln, possibly, or there is Clarence's son."

"He could never reign," she said fiercely. "Richard knows that."

The young earl would be eleven now, of an age, almost, with the dead Prince of Wales. The King had sent him North to the Neville stronghold of Sheriff Hutton, but Catherine remembered a terrified, backward child who could not yet sit on his pony and whose tantrums she had helped to soothe, granting him some protection from his drunken, infuriated sire. How little patience George of Clarence had had with his own son! The boy would always be slow to learn, needing constant care. No, he could not be looked to for the governing of England after King Richard.

"John of Gloucester is at Nottingham, I hear," Hugh said quietly. "That will be some comfort to his father, but his presence may rub more salt into the Queen's wounds, I fear."

John of Gloucester, Richard's natural son, conceived before his marriage to Warwick's Anne, was the child of a sewing maid he had favoured during his stay at his sister Margaret's Court of Burgundy during the dark months of 1470 while he fretted by Edward's side to return to England for the final battles for the throne. Then he had believed Anne lost to him, betrothed to the Lancastrian heir, who was later killed at Tewkesbury.

So many years ago, before Tewkesbury, before her father's execution. Catherine had never felt jealousy for the shadowy girl who had given John birth or for the mother of the Lady Catherine, his daughter. She had not known Richard then. He had been an enemy of the Lancastrian cause, whom her father had taught her to hate.

"You are not concerned — for young Richard?" Hugh had put his finger squarely on the agonizing doubt that assailed her.

"At supper Chauvet scarce took his eyes from the boy."

Hugh half turned in the dimness to peer into her eyes.

"Hugh, hold me tight. I could not bear it —" She drew a hard breath.

He made no answer and she knew he was blaming himself for the need that had caused her to reveal to the King the truth about her son. Now, if Richard should express a wish to have his child at Court, to be educated fittingly, even to acknowledge him, she would lose all rights over the boy. Well she knew such a procedure was common practice and that she and Hugh would be expected to feel honoured by such a decision on the King's part. Hugh made no attempt to give her false comfort, but stooped and kissed her, then held her close till she slept at last.

She came up with Perron Chauvet next morning in the hall as he was preparing to leave. He had not uttered the words she had dreaded. At breakfast he had eaten sparingly while he smilingly answered Janet's eager questions about the Court, but his eyes had again dwelt on young Richard, as if he would etch every line of the child's features onto his memory. Cecily had said little. She had had her taste of Court life and been glad to abandon it.

Chauvet turned now, as Catherine's gown rustled across the strewn rushes.

"Madame Catherine, I thank you for your hospitality." He touched his doublet. "I have safe your letter to Her Grace, the Queen."

She wasted no time in preamble. "Monsieur Chauvet, do you come to take my son from me?"

His green eyes flashed. "*Mondieu,* no. Why should you fear such a thing?"

"The King is bereft. He —"

"You know and trust him so little that you think he would take your own loved child from your care to comfort his loss? Madame Catherine," he chided gently, "fear has made you wrong him in your heart."

Her lips trembled and he took her hand. "I told you once before — on another matter, not to doubt him."

She smiled through her tears.

"You know so much of me, Monsieur, more than you should."

"You forget I tended you in your delirium."

"You have been watching the boy so carefully —"

"It is true that the King has asked for a detailed report on his son's progress and the state of his health. He will want to see him

— soon, but he will do nothing to hurt you or your husband and certainly not the boy."

"Thank you for coming so soon to tell us. Monsieur Chauvet —"

"Madame?"

"If I am needed, if there is ever anything at all I can do, you will find a way to tell me?"

He lifted her hand to his lips. "I will indeed, Madame, that I promise you."

Two

The chill, early months of May gave way to a fine June. The summer, this year, had been somewhat late in arrival and the villagers and servants on the manor took advantage of the lengthened days to tend their plots. Catherine felt very well and the baby thrived. She occupied herself in the pleasance and herb garden and was relieved to see Hugh once more immersed in manor business. During the winter and cold, wet spring, she knew he had fretted by his own fireside, longing to be with the Court at Newark, or Nottingham or on some errand for the King to Sheriff Hutton or Middleham. Cecily had returned to the convent at Tewkesbury, escorted by Rob Wentworth, in the second week of May and Janet pined for her company, the more so, since Richard escaped from his lessons with Father John whenever possible to be off fishing or riding his pony with Tom Walters.

In an effort to provide some diversion for

Janet, Catherine asked Hugh's permission to ride into Leicester with her younger step-daughter to buy materials for a birthday gown, ribbons and marten trimming.

Hugh had nodded absent-mindedly, his mind obviously engaged on the accounts which Jem, his steward, had presented to him only this morning.

"Certainly. Take Rob Wentworth. Do not spare the cost. It is time Janet thought of herself as a mature dame, perhaps an attractive gown will affect her behaviour."

Janet had flushed rosily and gone to her father's side to touch his velvet sleeve. She adored this stern-featured father, and knew well enough that, recently, Margery and Catherine had commented on her hoydenish ways. Had Cecily remained at home, she would have tempered her manners to suit her sister's orderly behaviour but there was no-one of an age at Kingsford to act as a confidante now she was approaching her thirteenth birthday. Catherine determined to spend more time with her. Ruefully she recalled that over the last months her attention, once over Hugh's peril, had turned on her coming lying-in, and more recently, on the welfare of her newly-born son and the management of the household, which always took on a state of frenzied activity at this time of year.

Both she and Janet rode well and enjoyed the journey but the heat caused the stinks of the open kennels to rise and they found the bustle of Leicester Town, once they had made their purchases, unpleasant and tiring, and gladly turned homeward.

Janet rode close, chattering eagerly about the mauve-coloured brocade and her first stylish hennin planned to compliment it. Catherine had taken Hugh at his word and also purchased for the girl a length of gold silk for a second gown.

As they entered the courtyard and Catherine stiffly allowed Rob to assist her to dismount she was aware of their groom holding a strange horse in readiness for some departing guest.

A sudden chill caused her to shiver lest a message from Court brought ill news as Chauvet had done so recently.

"So we have company?" Janet gazed down dismayed at the dust on her clothing and her dark eyes sought those of Catherine's in almost comic dismay. "Do we hasten to our chamber, Catherine, or will you present yourself in the hall?"

Before Catherine could consider her course of action the messenger, for so the man appeared to be, emerged from the house and strode towards his mount.

He was short, massive-chested like a wrestler, clad in leathern jack and dark hose. She recognized no familiar livery. As he passed them he touched his forelock respectfully enough but there was a faintly impudent air to the gesture as if it was made habitually from obsequious need rather than a genuine regard. The brow was low, his hair sandy under the woollen cap. She could not place the fellow, yet something about the close-set eyes and sloping chin roused a vague chord in her memory.

He rode off immediately and Catherine entered the house, paused only long enough in the hall to inform Hugh of their safe return, and then proceeded to assure herself that Baby Wilfred was sleeping content. Janet hurried to her chamber to change her gown for supper.

Wilfred was suckling at Luce's breast and obviously well. Catherine bent to kiss his silken, black head and, following Janet's example, went to her own chamber. Margery was stitching in the oriel embrasure by the dying rays of sunlight. Catherine reproved her gently.

"You try your eyes too much. You should be resting."

The older woman laid the small shirt aside. "That son of yours tears his clothes to shreds. I find it hard to keep pace with the mending. What a young rip he is, and Sir Hugh rarely disciplines him."

"Oh, you are a great one to talk, Margery," Catherine said, laughing. "Who feeds him with marchpane and gingerbread between meals? Not I nor Martine."

She allowed Margery to assist her into a fresh gown of blue silk.

"Did you enjoy the excursion, my lady? It is far to go for materials. What you needed could have been ordered at Bosworth."

"I know but Janet has so few outings," Catherine sighed. "She had hoped to take her place at Court as Cecily did, or, at least, to visit —" She did not complete the sentence. This was yet a further pricking reminder of Hugh's disgrace. "It was so busy in the town, market day and the swine market packed. We ate dinner at 'The White Boar'. However we were very satisfied by our purchases. You'll need to help us, Margery, if at least one of the gowns is to be ready for Janet to wear on her birthday."

"She's a good girl," Margery nodded, "if somewhat wild in her ways. She'd be climbing trees in the park still or fishing with the boys if I let her have her way, but she's always a civil tongue in her head and rarely loses her temper even at Richard's teasing."

"I see Sir Hugh received a messenger. Did you hear from whom?"

"No, my lady. I had an idea one came from Sir Richard Ratcliffe in Yorkshire but I didn't go down to enquire."

Ratcliffe had been in service with Hugh at Middleham waiting attendance on the King when he had then been Duke of Gloucester. Sir Richard remained one of the King's household gentlemen and continued to write to Hugh from time to time.

Janet was already down when Catherine arrived in the hall and was regaling her father with details of her promised finery.

"Would you consent to my wearing the pendant of seed pearls and rubies my mother left me?" She was leaning against his chair to refill his wine goblet, her tone wheedling.

"I should think I might, puss, if your conduct and demeanour assure me of your acceptance of your new state as lady of the household." He ruffled her dark hair with a gentle hand, smiling up at Catherine. His doublet was open and the shirt beneath and there was a beading of sweat on his forehead. Richard sat on a stool near the window, his narrow, dark face a mask of concentration on his Latin primer. He had left his books until it was too late to fish and was now attempting to learn passages set by long-suffering Father John. Catherine experienced a little pang of concern. How soon now before Hugh himself considered the boy old enough to enter the household of some lord of his acquaintance? Had Richard Ratcliffe been approached?

She waited until supper was concluded and the children in bed before asking about the Court news Hugh had received. It was still sultry and they lingered near the open oriel.

"I understand you had a dispatch from Ratcliffe. Is he still in attendance on the King?" She strove to keep her tone casual.

"Aye. The King has been at Scarborough to review the fleet and also some time at Pomfret."

"Then he still fears invasion by the Tudor?"

Henry Tudor's abortive attempt to land at Poole last October had failed with the defeat and capture of Harry of Buckingham.

Hugh shrugged. "He will be ever watchful of any such attempt."

"Does Sir Richard speak of Their Graces' health?"

"The King busies himself. I imagine that is some consolation but Ratcliffe's messenger tells me the Queen does not look well and grieves still, terribly, I suspect."

Catherine thoughtfully sipped her wine. "How dreadful that it should happen after the success of the King's first Parliament."

Master William Catesby had been elected Speaker in January. She recalled, with a little inward shudder, that the man had ever been at Crosby during the dark days of last spring before the execution of Lord William Hastings. She had been terrified for Hugh's involvement, since he had been friendly with the late King's chamberlain. She had been right to fear, since it had been an incautiously worded letter to Hastings, written by Hugh, which had caused the King to order his arrest and imprisonment in Warwick Castle. Catesby had been Hastings' man. Had he betrayed his master to his death? Clearly Lord William had treasonably intrigued with the Woodvilles against the Lord Protector and paid with his head.

Hugh said musingly, "Aye, the new laws will please the Commons but offend the nobility, at least those southern lords who do not know the King well yet."

Catherine agreed. Those measures which tightened up on the dangerously power-seeking practices of livery and maintenance of private armies would not be acceptable to men like Lord Thomas Stanley but the redressing of law concerning land tenure, the right to bail, and the abolition of forced loans, could only benefit Richard's poorer subjects. How agonizing for him now and a constant irritant that he must spare time and gold on the preparation for possible invasion.

"Ratcliffe writes that the King has bought twenty new guns and two serpentines for the Tower arsenal. Obviously he intends to take no chances."

"Sir Richard's man seemed in a great hurry to be gone. Has he urgent news to deliver further afield?" she asked curiously.

Hugh's eyes flashed, oddly. "Swayne is still with us. He is to ride out tomorrow."

"But I thought I passed the man in the courtyard as we rode in."

"That was another caller," Hugh commented grimly, "and one I had less wish to see here at Cadeby."

"He —"

Hugh bent and kissed her gently. "There is no need for you to worry your head, dear heart. I dismissed him, tail between his legs, to return to his master. He asked a favour of me I was not prepared to grant."

He rose and held out his hand to her. "Come, let us to bed. Even the short time you left me to-day I missed you sorely and welcome the sight of you home again."

His meaning was obvious and a scarlet flush mounted from her throat to her forehead. Willingly she went with him above stairs, for the moment the matter of the visitor forgotten.

It was still warm next morning but a fresher wind made it pleasant for riding and Hugh persuaded Catherine to accompany him to old Will Browne, their herdsman's cottage.

"He needs a new roof or urgent repair. I promised to ride over and inspect it. The old man has taken a bad chill a week ago and Joan, his daughter, tells me it has settled on his chest. Will you come, Catherine? He's fond of you and would appreciate a visit."

"Of course. I'll get some delicacies put up for him." She rose immediately from table to go to the buttery.

"May I come, my father?" Richard was already up and eager. "I am training my new greyhound to the leash. Please —"

"And your lessons?"

"Father John will be busied this morning. I am not to go to him till after noon."

Hugh shrugged, eyeing Catherine ruefully, as if she might wish to comment, then nodded. "Very well, but keep the whelp in check. Old Will won't want to cope with a boisterous pup or boy."

The lad rode well and Catherine noted how Hugh's eyes dwelt on him affectionately. Janet waved them off. Already she had no thoughts in her head other than to closet herself with Margery in the solar to make the first preparations for the fashioning of the new gown.

It was a pleasant journey and the old man was delighted to see her. She was relieved that

he seemed already over the worst and was becoming fractious and eager to return to his
work. After inspecting the roof and taking ale
with Will and his daughter while Richard
played happily outside with his hound whelp,
they prepared to return to the manor.

Catherine shaded her eyes against the sun
to gaze appreciatively at the long strips of
wheat and barley standing tall and green. If
the weather was dry during the harvest weeks
they should do excellently this year. At first
she thought that streak of light a trick of the
sun, then she heard Richard cry out and her
blood ran cold. She fought with her mount
to rein in and turn. Richard was only a short
distance behind Hugh, the hound running
close in behind. The arrow had pierced his
pony's flank and the poor, terrified beast was
rearing and threatening to throw the boy, the
hound whelp barking madly at its heels.
Hugh's behaviour seemed at that moment utterly astounding. Without thought for the
boy's plight he rode his hack straight for a
small clump of low scrub and young trees.

She rode back to Richard, calling to him
not to panic.

Excellent training from Hugh and Rob had
worked wonders. After the first fright he
had gathered his wits and calmed his infuriated mount and was reining him in and pat-

ting his shoulder.

"There, boy, there, steady, whoa, it's all right. We'll soon have you better."

Catherine dismounted with difficulty since there was none there to assist, and ran to him. She controlled an urge to gather him close as if he were a baby. It would be foolish to alarm him further.

"Are you hurt?"

"No, no, *mamon*, but my pony is hit. Oh, you do not think it is a bad wound?"

"No, no, I'm sure it is not." She steadied the pony and held out her arms to help Richard jump down. "Rob will know what to do."

With the boy held close, his eyes wide with wonder, she turned as Hugh came up to them, his eyes asking a terrible, silent question.

"We are perfectly safe," she reassured him. "What —" Her eyes slid to his dagger, as he bent to clean it on the grass. Richard's horrified gaze followed her own.

"I'm sorry. I had to get to him first, before I dared to even consider how badly —" He broke off grimly and called the dog sharply to heel then walked to the plunging pony Catherine was still struggling to control.

"It's torn a muscle, painful and frightening, but not too serious. Steady now," he soothed. "There's no cause for alarm, Richard, your pony will recover."

"The man — he's —" She gave a great, shuddering breath as her arm tightened round her son.

"Yes, he's dead."

"But who — *why*, Hugh?"

Not once had they experienced even a suspicion of hatred from any of their servants or villagers. The attack had come so suddenly and, apparently, without reason, that her knees threatened to buckle even yet and let her down, so close had the peril touched them all and spared them by a hairs-breadth of poor bowmanship.

"Sir Hugh?"

She looked up as Rob Wentworth topped a small rise ahead. A rush of relief swept over her. Rob, so dependable and close-mouthed when it was needful! She was grateful for reinforcements. Who knew whether their assailant had companions in hiding or more lying-in wait further off?

Now she saw he was carrying his bow. Rarely did he do that, only on Sundays when he practised at the butts with the rest of the household, as the law decreed.

Richard pulled away from her and ran to his pony. Rob shouldered his bow and hurried to examine the extent of the animal's injury.

She heard him reassure Richard as he carefully snapped off the feathered head of the shaft.

"Hush, little master, we'll take out the barb when we've got him back at the stable. He'll be carrying you again very soon."

She moved before Hugh could prevent her to the thicket where the dead man lay on his back, his eyes already glazed, staring upwards, that sandy hair dirt-stained now. Her eyes widened as she saw that Rob's arrow had struck him squarely in the chest before Hugh had needed to finish his work. It was more than likely that Rob's shot had deflected the man's aim and saved Richard. But how had Rob known? Her eyes sought Hugh's.

"Who is he?"

"He didn't give his name."

There was a note of grim humour in Hugh's tone and she trembled, fighting against hysteria.

"He could have killed Richard. There may be others who will try again. Dear God —"

"No, Catherine. It was me he wanted. He needed to silence me permanently."

She checked her panic to stare back at him, bewildered. "I don't understand. Why —"

"I told you. He came to me yesterday. An offer to a disaffected gentleman to transfer his allegiance."

"Treason?" She merely breathed the word.

"Henry Tudor would be prepared to offer me certain inducements."

"Then the fellow came from Brittany?"

"Ah, did he now?"

"We must send a report to the King immediately."

"No."

Again she regarded him blankly. "You must. To conceal this could put you in peril. The King *must* be informed."

"Catherine, we don't know who sent the man. I have no proof. His message was verbal."

"But the King cannot doubt you."

Hugh held her gaze and she read his concern. "The fellow is dead. I might well be deemed to say anything at this juncture in order to extricate myself from this coil. After all, I am by no means clear of suspicion." He hesitated. "In fact, yesterday, I was half convinced that I was being tested."

"You mean the King could have sent the man to trap you into complicity? Oh, no, Hugh."

"Or Lovell or — Stanley."

The name jarred her memory. She turned, shuddering, to the corpse. In the courtyard yesterday she had felt vaguely conscious of having seen him. Where? Her mind shied from the thought that it had been at Crosby or

Westminster. It was useless; she could not recall.

Rob strolled over, the dog still frisking round him, and gazed dispassionately at the body.

"It were best if you let me put this fellow below ground — privately, master."

"But there are bound to be enquiries about him," Catherine remonstrated distractedly, "especially if he came from —" She swallowed hard. "He may have companions."

"Not that he met since leaving Sir Hugh, yesterday," Rob said smoothly.

"You've kept him under watch?"

"Aye."

"I asked him to do so, Catherine. It's as well I did so."

Catherine turned to Rob. "Then you saw him conceal himself and lie in wait for us?"

"Aye. I followed him from 'The Lion' in Bosworth this morning."

"He could not have known where we were to go. Surely —"

Rob shrugged. "There is always talk in the inn. I couldn't get near enough to hear all he said to his drinking companions last night. Someone may have said, innocently enough, that you meant to visit old Will. It wouldn't be too difficult for him to discover where the old man's cottage was. I had a job keeping my distance from him. There's little cover near here. I saw him take aim too late to prevent it, but I dropped him before he could do further harm."

Catherine's gaze travelled to where Richard stood attempting to comfort his stricken pony.

"I must take the boy home."

"That would be best, mistress." Rob stirred the corpse with his foot. "You go home, master. Never fear. I'll get help to deal with this, help I can trust. I'll see he's interred decently with a prayer said over him."

Hugh nodded briskly, taking Catherine's arm. "Rob speaks sense, as ever. Come, my love, we mustn't further alarm Richard."

Indeed, Richard had come towards them now, as if anxious to investigate, and she was not willing that he should see the result of the men's handiwork. She hurried to him, turning him from the thicket.

"Mount with your mother, Richard," Hugh ordered. "I'll bring your pony home slowly. There's no cause for alarm."

"But —"

"You can see him in the stable the moment Rob and the farrier have extracted the barb."

Richard was inclined to argue but Hugh was firm and, at last, he lifted Catherine in to the saddle, put the boy before her, whistled the hound whelp and dispatched them to the manor, following behind himself, holding the pony's lead rein. She knew he would keep her in his sight even though the distance to Kingsford was slight.

It was difficult to behave as if nothing of note had occurred on their return to the house. Richard refused to enter until his pony was made comfortable and then Hugh insisted that the boy come to the solar. Slamming the heavy door to, he signalled for Richard to pour wine for himself and Catherine, seated himself and pulled the boy to him, placing the wine cup untouched on the table at his side.

"What happened this morning on the ride distressed you, Richard."

The boy nodded slowly. "Yes, my father."

"Alarmed you?"

Richard hesitated, frowned, then nodded again.

"There is naught to be ashamed of. I was afraid, not only for myself but for you and your mother."

"I understand."

"Now I am going to say something you will not understand and ask you to trust me."

Richard's frown deepened but his eyes continued to stare into Hugh's.

"I wish you to say nothing of what happened other than an accident, some villager aiming at a bird perhaps, shot your mount. The man has been punished, the matter is closed.”

Catherine held her breath. How could they expect a seven-year-old to realize their peril?

“Is the man dead, my father?”

“Yes.”

“Because he hates us? Did he wish to kill one of us?”

“Yes, me, Richard, because he feared me.”

“Because you are one of the King’s officers?”

“Yes, child.”

Richard nodded, and Hugh released his tight grip on the boy’s arm.

“I think I understand. There are always men who wish to kill the King and you are the King’s man?”

“Yes, Richard, I am truly the King’s servant.”

The boy looked reassuringly at Catherine. “You must not be frightened, *mamon,* Rob will deal with it all. He’s helped the farrier draw the barb from Roland’s flank. I held his head tight, even when he reared.”

She ruffled his dark hair. “We have to be very brave when we love someone or something a great deal. Roland will get well now.”

“I shan’t frighten Janet.”

“That would be best.”

He scampered off to coax sweetmeats from

Dame Alice Walters before going to the priest for his lessons.

Hugh prowled the solar, after draining the wine cup.

Catherine said, "Can we trust him not to babble of this to Tom?"

"I think we can."

She said slowly, "Whoever sent the man will become alarmed when he fails to report."

"You mean, should he in fact have come from the King, I shall be suspected of having disposed of one I thought to be a spy? I think not. Who is to say that he ever delivered his message or, indeed, reached Kingsford? He might well have met his death in some drunken brawl. If, as I think, he was off to Brittany, it may be long before he is missed."

"Then you believe him to be a courier between Henry Tudor and —"

"Ah, who?" He smiled thinly. "If I could be sure —"

"But why should you think the King would seek to trap you?"

He turned to her, his face in shadow, the oriel behind him.

"When his Grace issued his Commission of Array in May I sent immediately pleading for the privilege of serving him. I received a curt enjoinder to keep to my estates."

She caught back a little cry, knowing what

hurt he had felt on receiving such a rejection. His smile was rueful, his lip twisted.

"I was trusted, treated with affection. He will not now forgive me for criticizing his conduct."

"He cannot forgive you for doubting his motives."

Hugh made a regretful half bow.

"That may be so, and now, what if he distrusts mine?"

"Since the Hastings affair you have given him no cause to do so."

"There are those at his elbow who might wish to foster such a doubt."

She shook her head bewildered. "Catesby? You scarcely know the man. Lovell was your friend."

"Who puts the King's interests before everything, even his own safety."

"Lord Lovell told me your letter was placed into his hands and, in duty, he laid it before the King. Who could have seen that letter but — Lord Stanley?"

"Who indeed? Bishop Morton, or, of course, Catesby. He was, until that time, Hastings's man."

"One of them wishes you dead, Hugh, and for what other reason than to alienate another of the King's subjects from his side and render him further open to attack?"

"Aye, I know it."

"What can you do?"

He cupped her chin in his hands and bent to kiss her.

"Nothing, my love. We must watch and wait. I could wish I were closer to His Grace so I could draw more positive conclusions about the behaviour and motives of those in his confidence. At least Dick Ratcliffe keeps me informed."

"And you *do* trust him?"

"To the death." He stared at her shocked. "The man was my closest friend."

"Of course," she said, rising, forcing a smile, despite her forebodings. Hugh's last words bore an ominous ring.

Three

At the end of August, Catherine's feelings towards Hugh's former companions at Middleham were tested further when Sir Richard Ratcliffe rode over to visit them from Nottingham Castle. She greeted him in the courtyard with the customary stirrup cup and he gave her the kiss of greeting before they entered the house.

His presence soon dispelled all her doubts. He was a bluff, big man, hearty in manner, and the sound of that northern voice of his reassured her with memories of the old days at Richard's castle in the Yorkshire Dales.

"Hugh, it's good to set eyes on you again," he laughed, bowing to Janet who made him a respectful curtsey. "And who is this beauteous lady, I've never met? The Lady Janet? No, man, it cannot be. It *is?* Well, I can scarce believe it. As for you, Lady Catherine, two babes and as lovely as ever you were when you lamed poor Frank Lovell's horse that day." He laughed at the memory. "It seems the world has turned upside down since then. Thank you, boy." This to Richard who served him with wine. "You've a comely page, Hugh. No mention of him in your letters."

"My son does not grow over-tall for his age but his manners improve, Sir Richard," Hugh said, proudly.

Catherine felt that familiar prickle of doubt as Ratcliffe wiped his mouth with his hand and stared after the boy in open curiosity.

"So this is my namesake. A fine boy, indeed, Hugh. The King has not seen him yet, I take it, Lady Catherine?"

"Unfortunately not yet." Catherine's tongue almost clove to the roof of her mouth. This man was one of the King's closest friends. Did he know, suspect? He it was who had called them awake on the morning when the Duke and she had consummated their love. Had he been sent on yet another errand of enquiry, concerning the health and progress of the King's son?

"And the babe thrives?"

"Yes, you must see him. But, forgive me, Sir Richard, you may not have the desire to look at babies."

"Indeed I have the greatest wish to see this boy you've borne Hugh," he said heartily. "I would have come before but you know I've been busied on the King's affairs." He gave an awkward cough as if excusing himself from the oblique reference to Hugh's banishment from Court.

"How are the King and Queen in health?" she asked.

The smile faded from Ratcliffe's eyes. "She is not well, poor lady. She has not, alas, the press of affairs which keeps Richard from dwelling too torturously on his own grief."

Catherine nodded and drew Janet and Richard to the window, leaving the two men at table. Richard obediently bent his head over his Latin primer while Janet needed no prompting to look to her stitching. She was hemming a new veil for her hennin. Catherine busied herself attaching seed pearls to the velvet of the frontal, but she could hear the men's talk clearly enough.

"You heard that the King has ordered the re-interment of King Henry's body in Windsor?"

Hugh was clearly astounded. "It has been moved from Chertsey?"

"Aye. The King considered Windsor more fitting poor King Hal's royal state. The chapel of St. George is almost completed. King Henry will lie on the south side of the altar, the late King Edward on the north, as you know."

"Is he aware that the rumours concerning King Henry's death —" Hugh had lowered his tone and Catherine strained her ears to catch Sir Richard's answer.

"You know His Grace. He will not so much as trouble himself to repudiate them. You and I know well that on the night of the King's death Richard was with us in Kent hunting the Bastard Fauconberg."

Hugh himself poured more wine for his guest.

"How long will the Court be in Nottingham?"

"Who knows? The King confers with the Scots. There is talk of a proposed marriage between the King's niece, Anne de la Pole, the daughter of his sister, the Duchess of Suffolk, and James's eldest son, the Duke of Rothesay."

"So peace seems certain on the Border. What of the Tudor?"

Catherine heard Ratcliffe give the throaty, deep chuckle she well remembered. "That Welsh fox has got clear away to France."

"He has left Brittany?"

"Aye. He must have got wind that Richard had arranged with the Breton envoys at his meeting with them at Pontefract in June to return our Henry to more careful custody. Apparently he was at Vannes with his uncle, Jasper of Pembroke, and some three hundred followers. Uncle Jasper leaves Vannes to consult with Duke Francis, then he turns south and makes for Anjou. Meanwhile our wily nephew, who, I understand, is constantly watched, rides out of Vannes only two days later to visit some friends, or so he averred. No-one doubted since he took only a handful of servants. Suddenly he goes missing and turns up in France where, it appears, he had already been promised refuge. In all events the French King refuses to return him to Landois's custody or ours. Henry must have thrown off pursuit by changing his clothes during the journey."

"That's a blow for Richard."

"Worrying to have the man at large, especially now, since the posting of that infamous rhyme on the door of St. Pauls, and, of course, Morton is still intriguing abroad. It was mad of Richard not to have clapped the man in the Tower after the Hastings affair."

"Rhyme? What rhyme?"

"I forget you are out of touch here in the wilds of Leicestershire. I have to confess the thing had a note of grim humour though Frank Lovell does not see it that way and burns to get his hands on Will Colyngbourne."

"Colyngbourne, you mean the Duchess Cecily's man?"

"Colyngbourne who *was* the Duchess Cecily's man. He's been in hiding since Christmas, believed to have been in treasonable correspondence with Buckingham. Sorry, Hugh, I touch on a festering wound."

"No matter. What did this rhyme say?"

Catherine's heart leaped to her throat. Had the man dared to accuse or even imply that Richard had harmed his nephews?

"It was in doggerel and ran:
'The Cat, the Rat, and Lovell, Our Dog,
'Ruleth all England under a Hog'."

Hugh gave a sharp exclamation and Janet jerked up her head in shocked surprise.

Hugh gave a grim laugh. "Faith, Dick, he does not flatter any of you. God help him if he's caught."

"He'll more than likely have fled to France to join the Tudor by now unless he's fool enough to remain attempting to turn loyal men from their allegiance."

Catherine thanked the saints that Ratcliffe was unable to read her heart at that moment. Her mind went guiltily to the secret grave somewhere on the manor into which Rob had bundled the corpse of the unknown messenger. Had he come from Colyngbourne — or from Colyngbourne's master?

Ratcliffe stayed one night with them. He dandled little Wilfred and accompanied young

Richard to the stables to see his pony, Roland, and the hound whelp, took an interest in Hugh's continuing alterations and additions to the house, and took his departure, jovially promising to keep them informed of future developments at Court.

His smile faded for one moment before he prepared to ride out. "Be sure that I wait only for the right opportunity to speak to the King on your behalf, Hugh."

"I know that, old friend."

Hugh seemed more cheerful after Ratcliffe had gone and returned to his duties about the manor with renewed enthusiasm. He laughed off Catherine's fears for the King's safety.

"My dear, this scurrilous attack on him in the rhyme is nothing new. Each King wears his crown uneasily. You know that only too well. There are those with Lancastrian leanings still and others who hanker for power and those land-crazy who see opportunities only in treason. Richard will know how to deal with these threats. The failure of Buckingham's venture showed the landed gentry who is master in England."

"Yet there is always Henry Tudor spinning his web now at liberty out of the reach of the King's allies. If Elizabeth Woodville were to correspond with him she could gain support. She will never forgive Richard for acting so speedily and crushing her attempts to take power into her own hands and the deaths of Lord Rivers, her brother and her son, Dick Grey, are to be reckoned to her account against the King."

"Yet it seems she *has* forgiven him. She has come out of the Westminster Sanctuary with her daughters in acceptance of the King's most solemn pledge to keep them all in safety and provide for their future. She has even written to Dorset advising him to come home and trust to the mercy of the King, though he has been prevented from doing so by Henry, naturally."

"But if Elizabeth believes that the King has harmed her sons —" Catherine twisted the belt of her gown nervously. "Doesn't it seem odd behaviour, Hugh, in a loving mother?"

Hugh grinned mirthlessly. "I have yet to have proof that Elizabeth is indeed a 'loving mother' rather than a scheming one. That is to say, of course, she does not want for some natural affection but she will always put her lust for power first. For all that, surely her behaviour now in putting her trust in the King proves once and for all that she is knowledge-able about the welfare of her boys. Even Eliz-abeth would not accept money from the hands of a man she believes to have murdered her sons."

Catherine nodded thoughtfully. She had met

that famed beauty during the short time she had been in attendance at Edward's Court. Venal the Dowager Queen might be and ready to use her children as pawns in the game of power, as Hugh had said, but she loved them. She must know where the boys were, corresponded with them, perhaps. Without clear proof of Richard's innocence concerning Edward's sons she would not have agreed to emerge from Sanctuary for, if the King were ruthless enough to have disposed of the Princes, what faith could she have that their sisters would not have followed them to their graves? No, Elizabeth must be sure, and Catherine herself had been reassured by Chauvet on that matter.

It was when the Burgundian's arrival was announced in October that she guessed, this time, at his reason. She was alone in the solar, Janet and Richard out hawking with their father. Silently he handed her a sealed package.

The letter was short in the Queen's own hand.

"Catherine,

"If your children thrive and can manage without you for a while, would you come to me? I need you, would find comfort in your presence.

"Anne."

She had not even used the 'R' of Regina. This was a plea from one friend to another. Catherine had spent few actual days in the Queen's service either at Middleham or last year when as Duchess of Gloucester she had travelled from the North to join her husband at Crosby Hall, but, from the beginning, when Anne had taken her into service from the nunnery at Tewkesbury, there had been a special bond of affection between them. Both had lost fathers in the Wars, both had depended on the good offices of Richard of Gloucester. Catherine had always guiltily feared that Anne was aware that both of them loved him.

She looked up now at Perron Chauvet. "I will come, of course. Hugh will understand the need. The baby will be in good hands and is thriving."

"It will not be for long."

She paled and he shook his head gently.

"Does the King know that — that she is dying?"

"He cannot fail to know. The physicians have forbidden him her bed for fear of him taking the contagion." He smiled faintly. "I do not think he always keeps to their advice but, *naturellement,* she is too sick most of the time. The death of the boy has finished her, I fear. If we take precautions I do not believe there will be great harm to your health."

"That cannot be helped if it is so. She has asked for me. I would not refuse even if she were not the Queen. Do we ride to Nottingham?"

"Yes, but the King intends to remove his Court to London early next month. He will celebrate Christmas in his capital and there is little fear of invasion now until the Spring of next year."

"Can we wait to leave until the morning? There are arrangements to be made."

"Certainement."

She called for attendants to see to hospitality for their guest over night and went in search of Margery Whittacker.

The older woman made no objection to Catherine's expressed wish for her to remain with the children. Though she would have preferred to be in attendance on her mistress she knew well enough where her duty lay.

"You can rest easy, mistress. I shall summon you home if there is the least fear that one of the children has need of you. Will you take Martine?"

Catherine grimaced. Though a good-hearted girl, Martine had not the strength of character or experience on which she could lean in any emergency and she needed someone utterly reliable during these coming weeks of separation from Hugh and the household.

"If Sir Hugh is agreeable I shall take only Rob and Maud," she said hastily.

Rob Wentworth had married Maud Daly only three weeks ago. Catherine had been delighted for Maud had been the cause of her salvation last October, taking her place in the household and momentarily fooling the King's captain, Jehan Trêves, long enough to allow Catherine to reach Hugh and warn him of his impending arrest. Maud was practical and dependable. No-one would be better for the purpose. Catherine would have little time to keep her eyes on a possibly flighty maidservant.

Hugh gave his consent for the journey and added his approval of her choice of attendants. Janet pleaded to accompany her.

"Child, I cannot appoint you to the Queen's household without her leave," Catherine explained. "Since I go to attend the Queen in sickness I shall have few opportunities to visit you if I have to leave you in some inn and there would be the need to take another girl to attend you, which would leave Margery short-handed here. I shall send for you later if I need you and there is much you can do here. Margery will have her hands full with the baby and I shall require you to order the household servants." Janet was mollified by Catherine's opinions of her capabilities and made no more protests.

Catherine detected in Hugh's love-making that night a note of hungry desperation. Lying cradled in his arms she twisted dark locks of his hair between her fingers.

"Trust me, Hugh. I shall not become the King's mistress. All that is over."

He cupped her face in his hands and kissed her tenderly. "My love, I cannot bear to be without you, yet I know you must go."

"Chauvet says it cannot be for long," she said, soberly.

Hugh gave a little sigh. "Poor Dickon, first the boy now Anne."

"Her message was urgent. I am not sure how I can be of assistance."

"She remembers your nursing skill while you worked with the infirmarian at Tewkesbury, perhaps."

"I think there is more behind her call to me than that."

He said quietly, "Be cautious. Remember that not all women who attend on the Queen have her best interests at heart."

"I know it."

"There have been no repercussions to the affair of the messenger."

"You still think someone at Court, close to Richard, dispatched the man?"

"Aye." He tightened his hold of her, kissing the heavy tresses of hair lying soft on her neck and shoulder. "I'm glad Rob Wentworth will be with you."

"I shall keep you informed."

"Do, but be discreet in what you write. Messengers can be intercepted."

She lay wakeful for hours after Hugh slept. It seemed now she was returning to the intrigue-ridden coterie of the Court. For months Kingsford had been a quiet haven, a safe nest in which her little son had been born in happiness. Before, when she had ventured among the bejewelled throng who walked the corridors of Westminster, the lust for power behind the masked obsequiousness of courtesy and manners, she had had Hugh by her side. Now she must face that veiled enmity alone. She snuggled into a more comfortable posture and, as she slipped into final slumber, she saw before her eyes, the handsome mocking countenance of Perron Chauvet. Indeed, the man could match guile with guile and Chauvet, she knew, would guard *her* interests.

Four

Catherine was heartened by her first sight of the Queen. Anne had already put off complete mourning and was dressed in a gown of heavy purple velvet trimmed with ermine. Her hennin was decorated in silver thread with seed pearls. Though the delicate bones of her face were tight pulled under the flesh and Catherine saw that she had lost more weight than she could afford, for she had always been slight made, the gown appeared to hang heavy on those slender shoulders, she had not that look of exhaustion Catherine had expected. The cheeks flushed with delight and the very blue eyes sparkled as she welcomed her former attendant with the kiss of greeting.

"Catherine, I had not expected you so soon. The children, they are well?"

"Very well, Your Grace. I hope I see you better, for Monsieur Chauvet tells me you have been indisposed."

"My cough troubles me again with the onset

of Autumn but I am improving now, the more so since I have you with me."

She dismissed her ladies and Catherine drew up a stool to sit close to her near the fire. She was hesitant to mention the terrible cause of the Queen's sorrow and, at last, Anne took it upon herself to broach the matter, putting one hand gently on Catherine's arm.

"We laid him to rest at Sheriff Hutton. Richard has plans for a splendid tomb. It seemed most fitting that he should remain in the North where — where we had all been happy together. You must not mind, Catherine, if I insist on talking to you about him. My ladies avoid the subject, thinking it will distress me, but I cannot shut him out, forget him."

"Madam, I had not known how to —"

"I know. My confessor tells me it is the will of God and that I must bear the loss bravely. I know it and would face it more courageously if there had been hope of other children — but that is not possible. Only to you can I say what is in my heart. I have failed Richard. He has lost more than his son. His heir was the visible sign of the continuity of his line, his successor, now he is laid open further to the malice of his enemies and his fears for the peace of the realm grow daily. He has never reproached me —"

"Madam, he loves you with all his heart. You must believe that and take it for your comfort."

"Catherine, I know how he loves me." The Queen's blue, almost violet, eyes misted with tears and she looked away. "When — when he took me from Sanctuary I feared him. *I* feared *him*. Oh, I can smile now at the thought, he who has always treated me with true affection and courtesy, but, you see, I was a pawn used by my father, though he, too, professed to love me well, then by Queen Margaret and by George of Clarence —" She broke off as if the memory of those terrible days following the Lancastrian defeat at Tewkesbury was too great for her to recount or bear. "He looked so grim then and unyielding, my Richard, and he took me home after the marriage to Middleham. If only you could understand how I long to return."

"I understand, madam."

"Young John of Gloucester is a great comfort to me. Had he been arrogant, thrown in my face his — his right to be at the King's side, I would have found his presence at Court unbearable, but he is a good boy with great affection for the King."

"I have never seen him. Does he resemble the King?"

"No, he is very fair, Neville fair. They say,

surprisingly, that he resembles me — as Edward did." The rosy flush again dyed her cheeks. "Richard always preferred women with light hair."

Catherine's heart missed a beat and she dared not face the Queen's gaze.

"I have sent for you because — we both love him dearly, Catherine. There are more way of injuring a monarch than by treasonable correspondence, intrigue, the knife or poisoned wine. These perils threaten Richard now and I would have you by me that we can fight them together and that you might continue to do so — after I have gone."

"Madam —"

"Catherine, I shall speak of this once now and then not again until it is time. I know you love my husband. I also know how loyal you are to me — and to Hugh. I cannot explain yet how I believe you can help by your presence here." She gave a little shaky laugh. "I do not ask that you become the King's mistress. You will soon see for yourself how things are and know what it is I fear. He has true affection for you. You hold to the old loyalties. Lovell, Ratcliffe, Rob Percy, Brackenbury; they all know and trust you, and will turn to you to intercede for them with the King when there is need. Do I ask too much, just now when your son is so small?"

"No, my dear lady, of course you do not. My children are in good hands. I promise I will stay while you need me. In the spring, when your health improves, I shall go home to them."

A faint smile glimmered on Anne's lips and she shook her head regretfully. "We shall see. Perhaps." Then more briskly, "The royal children are at Sheriff Hutton. I miss them all."

That simple word 'all'. Did she speak of the King's nephew, young John of Lincoln and of the Earl of Warwick? Or did she think of those other, shadowy beings, never mentioned now at Court, Edward's sons?

Catherine had been away from Court scarcely a year, yet, already, her quiet existence at Kingsford made the splendour of the banquet in the great hall of Nottingham Castle seem alien to her; the smell of the heavily spiced, rich dishes, the rowdy bawdiness, the music from the gallery almost drowned out by the shouts of applause for the King's jester, and the jugglers. She sat among the Queen's ladies but felt alone in that vast, raftered place lit by the torches and jewel-like colours and glitter of the brilliantly clad ladies and nobles who surrounded her. Richard and his Queen sat remote from her under the great cloth of estate. From time to time Catherine saw him turn to his Queen solicitously, though he was entertaining embassies from Burgundy and Scotland and forced to give to them his courteous attention.

The attendant ladies obviously regarded her with veiled curiosity. The lady Margaret, Clarence's daughter, was not among them. Catherine had herself attended on the Queen briefly from May last year until after the coronation, but several of them had been newly appointed. They questioned her politely about Sir Hugh and the children, but she felt that they were secretly wondering why she had been summoned now and the warmth with which the Queen had received her would win her no favour in their eyes. Already she was accounted to be the Queen's confidante and they would be wary of what words they uttered in her presence.

Her eyes scanned the board for those among the King's gentlemen she knew. Lovell she immediately recognised, once more closest to the King's side now that Buckingham had paid the supreme price for his bid for power. Sir Richard Ratcliffe acknowledged her presence with a nod and came to her side when the feasting was over and the dancing commenced. He was somewhat insistent on taking the floor with her.

"I regret the inconvenience if you do not

wish to dance, Catherine. It is just that nowadays it is the safest place for us to talk, when all eyes are on us. How is Hugh?"

"Well, and the children. The queen has asked for me —"

"Yes, I know, and am glad of it."

"Why —" Her eyes scanned his serious face, usually so hearty and jovial. She was not sure what he meant by the brief comment but before she could say anything further the music came to an end and, as Sir Richard prepared to lead her back to her place, a page presented himself, bowing low.

"His Grace, the King, commands your attendance, Lady Kingsford."

Her heart pounded as she approached the King's chair. She had not seen him since that frightening audience last October. As always their meetings were bitter-sweet, his nearness a torment, for loving Hugh as she did, a dutiful wife, the first flowering of passion had been for this man, and it had never diminished. She had known that one night as she had lain clasped in his arms she would love him until they were both in their graves.

Like the Queen he had put aside mourning and was resplendent in purple velvet and cloth of silver. She curtseyed low, the betraying flush hidden from him and the Queen by her hennin's veiling.

"Catherine, as ever, it is good to welcome my ward to Court. Now I am free of my duties as sovereign and host for a while I would take the floor with you."

Her heart fluttered at the touch of his fingers as he guided her in the dance. If, as rumour said, he had been injured as a child and one shoulder raised slightly higher than the other, and one leg fractionally shorter, he showed no sign of it in the dance, nor, she knew to her cost, in his prowess on the battlefield. Much smaller and slighter than his magnificent elder brother, he was still a splendid figure, springing nimbly and elegantly to the minstrel's music. As the dance concluded he drew her aside, as Ratcliffe had done, to the side of the hall.

"Let us stroll from the heat of the hall, Catherine," he said his hand under her elbow.

She went at his command, and, at last, he drew her to a halt into a deserted oriel embrasure, the light of the two brands in their sconces illuminating his face.

He looked stern as he always did, older than his thirty-one years. She looked up fully now they were no longer observed to scan his features anxiously. His latest, terrible grief was limned there, for all to see, but that tight mouth was smiling and his normally pale features, rosy with the exertion of the dance. He bent and kissed her fingers.

"It was good of you to come so soon, and after the birth of the child. She has suffered so terribly. You will be good for her. These women protocol demands that she have round her —" His mouth tightened again. "My welcome is no empty courtesy, Catherine, you must know that."

"I know it." Her answer was a whisper.

"How is my boy?"

"In excellent health and spirits, inclined to neglect his studies for hawking and fishing." She smiled, "Yet he is a good boy, my lord, loving and courteous. I believe you will be proud of him."

"Please God, I may see him soon. And the other children, Hugh's daughters and the baby?"

"All well. Cecily has returned to the nunnery at Tewkesbury. You will recall Hugh went there —"

"I remember," he said his smile a little grim. It had been to chase his errant daughter that had taken Hugh from the King's side during the Rising last year and heightened suspicions of his treason.

There was a little silence while she sought for words to frame what was in her heart.

"My dear lord I am so deeply sorry for your

loss of the Prince — and of His Grace of Buckingham."

There was a strange flash to those grey-
green eyes and he inclined his chin briefly.

"Ah, Catherine, how well you understand
me. Do you know, not one of my intimates,
have said such words to me."

"If I offend —"

"You do not." Momentarily a suspicion of
tears glinted in his eyes. "I loved Harry Stafford well. He reminded me of George. Ah
well, we must put such thoughts aside. I have
learned to be ruthless in these last days. My
Edward would have made a just, kindly ruler,
but ruthlessness was not in his nature. It is
doubtful if he would have survived long on
the Throne."

" 'Ruthless' is not the word I would use,
my lord."

His lips curved wryly. "You will be kind
to me then and term the necessity, 'kingly
strength', Catherine?"

"And so it is, sir." Firmly she turned the
subject against his need for self blame. "The
Queen tells me Prince Edward lies at Sheriff
Hutton."

"Aye, his tomb will be lovingly tended there
where they love him well. I have given orders
for the commission of it. It shall be of ala-
baster, bearing his effigy in his robes and cor-

onet as Prince of Wales."

A hard lump formed in her throat. "I shall never forget him so bravely riding his pony at Middleham."

"Nor the townsfolk of York his ceremonial entry into the city when he was created Prince of Wales. It was a proud moment for us all."

He reached out and took her hand. "We leave soon for Westminster. I want you to tell me, Catherine, if the Queen is over-fatigued by any part of the journey. She will not complain or ask to go more slowly. Daily she seeks to hide her condition from me, which is courageous but absurd. Hobbes is now back from Yorkshire and she is in his charge. She likes and has confidence in him." His voice broke harshly. "He has told me just how seriously ill she is, so you must hide nothing from me. The other ladies would not dare to disobey her. I can rely on you?"

Catherine nodded. "My training in the convent infirmary at Tewkesbury will stand me in good stead. Trust me, sir. I will know when to summon Dr Hobbes and when it is needful to inform you of any sudden change in the Queen's condition."

They were intent on their talk and did not notice the sudden swish of brocaded skirts across the flagged floor which heralded the arrival of another. Catherine pulled away from the King's grasp awkwardly as she heard a betraying hiss of breath, and, turning, saw a young woman exquisitely dressed and bejewelled, who immediately sank into a low curtsey.

"My lord uncle, forgive me. I did not realize you were engaged in private talk."

"Bess." He smiled as she rose and indicated Catherine. "You perhaps may not remember Lady Catherine Kingsford. Your father gave me her wardship long ago after Tewkesbury. Catherine, the Lady Elizabeth Plantagenet."

It was Catherine's turn to sink low in a curtsey.

The Lady Elizabeth's voice was somewhat chilled. "I do, indeed, recall that the Lady Catherine attended my mother. I trust you will be happy at Court, Lady Kingsford. You have a very small baby, I hear."

Catherine was at a loss to understand the lady's hostility. There was no mistaking that look of hauteur, yet Catherine remembered Edward's children as pleasing-mannered, without condescension to subjects, like their father.

In appearance the late King's eldest daughter was very like her famed beautiful mother, though decidedly plumper. Only a suspicion of hair could be glimpsed from beneath the frontal of her jewelled hennin but Catherine judged her fair. The eyes were blue, and just now her mouth was held in a petulant pout, soon to relax into the semblance of a smile as she understood the King's desire that she should greet Catherine warmly. Her foot, in its jewelled slipper, tapped impatiently on the flagstones as if she were anxious to return to the lights and merriment of the great hall.

Catherine felt an answer was called for. She lowered her gaze respectfully. "Yes, I leave my baby son at Cadeby in excellent hands, I praise the Virgin. It was a wrench to leave him just now but Her Grace wrote that she had need of me. I am grateful for your courteous welcome, Lady Elizabeth."

Richard smiled. "What did you want, Bess? Is Anne asking for me?"

"No, no, of course not." His niece coloured. Catherine thought that fair skin would often be marred by floridness, particularly in moments of stress. Clearly the Lady Elizabeth betrayed her displeasure at seeing the King in talk with his ward withdrawn from the press of courtiers. She felt herself flushing hotly in response.

Elizabeth turned her very blue eyes on her uncle. "You will recall, my lord, you promised to dance with me but clearly you are instructing Lady Catherine in her duties."

The King shook his head. "We have finished our discussion. I *had* forgotten but only momentarily." He gave Lady Elizabeth's head-dress a teasing tweak. "Certainly I will dance with you. It always gives me great pleasure, you are such an excellent partner, Bess."

He gestured for both ladies to accompany him back to the hall.

"Lady Catherine has had experience of nursing. We are grateful to have her in attendance on the Queen and mindful of her sacrifice in leaving her family."

The regal 'we' seemed a tacit reminder that Catherine was summoned to Court on his orders and was to be treated with marked courtesy.

As the King moved to the throne dais to rejoin the Queen before dancing with his niece, Catherine once more drew back into a respectful curtsey as the former princess was about to pass her. Again those blue eyes dwelt on her coldly and Catherine was aware that, for some reason she could not yet gauge, she had come under the lady's undoubted displeasure.

Five

The Court was re-established in Westminster Palace by the ninth of November and Catherine, who had stayed close to the Queen's side throughout the journey, was relieved to report regularly to the King during its course that she was standing up to its rigours well. On occasions Anne insisted on abandoning her richly caparisoned horse-litter and riding by her husband's side. Catherine wondered if the very act of leaving Nottingham, where the dread news of her son's death had first reached her, had heartened the Queen, for, despite her reiterated desires to be back in the North, which practicality told her was patently impossible, she seemed pleased to be once more settled in her own apartments and began to speak of preparations for the Holy Season of Christmas, now only weeks away.

"It must be cheerfully observed this year, above all others," she told her ladies. "We have had our fill of sorrow and our festivities shall mark a new beginning of better times in store."

Catherine was installed in a small chamber close to the Queen's apartments with Maud Wentworth occupying the truckle bed alongside.

Rob had taken himself into the city and obtained a lodging at 'The Crossed Keys' in Chepeside where Catherine and Hugh had established their household last year when they had returned to England from Burgundy.

Catherine had been apologetic about the need to so soon part the newly-married couple but Maud had briskly put aside the inconvenience.

"Never bother yourself about that, mistress. The lodging in Chepeside is only a suitable base to stable our horses and equipment." She grinned saucily. "Most of the time Rob is here and sleeps where he can in the hall or with the grooms. When he wants me he lets no discomfort stand in his way. Besides, he has Sir Hugh's instructions to keep a watchful eye on your welfare. I gather Mistress Ruislip is used to his ways and can be trusted to keep our belongings securely."

"Indeed she can and is as discreet as any innwife one would hope to meet." Catherine sighed as Maud adjusted her hennin. "While I am glad to be of service to Her Grace I shall be happier when I am back with the children and I dread the thought of Christmas away from them."

"You had fine tidings of them all before we left Nottingham, mistress. That's a great comfort. Lord," Maud grimaced comically at the noise from the corridor as two young pages whooped by, bellowing derisive comments at each other, "if only this place was quieter. Can we not ask the King's Grace to give instructions about it? The Queen, poor lady, would rest easier without this racket."

"I'll see to it," Catherine promised grimly.

Fortunately Anne's cough had not troubled her so much these recent nights, but should she need to rest in the day this constant commotion must not be allowed to continue.

Maud proved an invaluable waiting maid, though Hugh had laughingly doubted her ability.

"Poor Catherine," he had grinned. "Maud has undoubted talents but none likely to be useful to you, my love, save that I must admit she is capable in emergencies and knows how to keep a close tongue. Don't let her brighten your hair. I prefer it as it is."

They had laughed ruefully together at Maud's delight in her brassily golden locks, lightened with cow's urine. Now, in her newly married state, she hid her former glory discreetly under wimple and cap.

Surprisingly Maud had revealed a deftness and skill in cleaning and preparing Catherine's gowns and linen, also dressing her hair. Her expertise with the tweezers in keeping the eyebrows in line was remarkable. Catherine had resisted the newest fashion of shaving the front of her hair to add to the height of the brow. Her pale, glossy front hair showed in a smooth band as it always had. Hugh preferred it so and Catherine wondered fleetingly about the Queen's odd remark.

'Richard ever preferred women with light hair.'

She was somewhat puzzled on entering the antechamber to the Queen's bedroom one morning in late November to find the attendant ladies gathered into a little frightened huddle. Catherine's heart gave a sudden leap of alarm. Was the Queen worse? She had been pleasurably tired but in good spirits when she had retired last night and Catherine had sat by her bed for an hour reading to her from one of Master Caxton's latest printings of a Book of Hours, a gift from the King. No-one had summoned her to the Queen's side during the night when another lady had kept watch. Surely she would have been informed of any matter for concern.

"What is wrong?" she asked abruptly.

These days she paid little attention to the fact that the other ladies did not readily seek her company.

Four pairs of eyes regarded her, rounded with curiosity, even a trace of animosity, but she detected no cause for alarm. Recently she had become accustomed, deeming the King's orders implicit, to take responsibility for making decisions concerning the Queen's welfare.

"You look nervous. Is Her Grace unwell?"

"No, no." Mary Winton, round-faced, kind-hearted but somewhat inefficient, fiddled awkwardly with her girdle. "The Queen has not yet rung her bell."

"If there is ill news to relate to the Queen you'd best tell me now. I know how you all are anxious to avoid upsetting her."

"The news is not ill — for the Queen," Isobel, Mary's younger sister, put in pertly. "It would depend on what sympathies you held, as to how one considered it."

"Your sympathies are with the Queen, I would have thought," Catherine retorted tartly.

There was a nervous murmur of assent.

"Well, what is it?" she snapped, exasperated. "Some gossip is obviously filling your thoughts to the detriment of your duties. The Queen's toiletries should be laid ready and —"

Isobel's wide-eyed expression took on an

appearance of self-satisfaction, since her knowledge so clearly exceeded Catherine's.

"That man is caught at last. The trial is fixed for November twenty-ninth."

"That man?"

"Colyingbourne, of course. He who wrote that shameful verse." Isobel's cheeks flushed, whether from embarrassment or the secretly malicious amusement at another's discomfiture Catherine could not be sure.

"Indeed?" Catherine's reply was uncompromisingly blunt and did not invite further comment but it was forthcoming.

"He called the King a hog." The girl's voice sank to a whisper. "One of the pages said the trial is to be at the Guildhall and the King has appointed a great commission to hear the case under the Dukes of Norfolk and Suffolk, Viscount Lovell and —"

"The man will surely be charged with treasons more deadly than some scurrilous rhyme and the King ensures by such a proceeding that the trial will be a fair one. But this does not concern us. Listening to pages' gossip is unworthy of you, Isobel. I'll wake the Queen so get you to your work and let no talk of this disturb Her Grace. You know very well she has so gentle a heart that she will be dreadfully sorry for the prisoner's suffering if he *is* convicted, despite his vitriolic attacks on the

King's reputation."

The little group drew apart reluctantly as Catherine passed into the bedchamber. She was frowning. Unfortunate, that now the atmosphere of the Court had lightened with the promise of the Christmas festivities and the Queen heartened, this cloud of poisonous doubt and suspicion would darken it again.

The King arrived during the final stages of the Queen's toilet. Catherine saw that he held his mouth in tightly, a sign of strain in him she knew well, but he greeted his wife cheerfully, drawing her into a close embrace.

"I shall be busied throughout the day, my love, and may not be able to dine with you. Please excuse the need which keeps me from your side."

"The clothier is to come today, Richard," she reminded him smiling rosily, "with materials for my new gown. I may spend freely?"

"Aye, love." He dropped a final kiss on her forehead. "We've had few occasions recently to rejoice. Choose whatever takes your fancy. I swear I'll not deem you over extravagant."

Anne had thrown herself headlong into these preparations and her talk throughout the morning was of nothing else. If she had heard mention of the coming trial, which Catherine doubted, she made no mention of the fact and was delighted when the merchants from the Chepe arrived to display their wares.

The sight of the beautiful cloths excited the attention of all the ladies, dispelling the gloom of outside events, and they gave little cries of admiration as bolts of blue and green velvet, cloth of gold, brocades in pinks, silver and blues were undone and draped across chairs, stools and carpet for the Queen's approval.

With a reckless disregard for economy Anne made presents to her ladies of these bolts for which each expressed admiration. She beckoned Catherine forward.

"Now, which for you? You will wish, perhaps, to visit Kingsford for Christmas, I know, but you must have a new gown for the occasion. Come and choose."

"Your Grace, your gracious permission for me to visit the children is gift enough."

"Nonsense," Anne laughed, "I shall want to see you soon in my gift. Blue — or this rose velvet? This would become you excellently." She draped the deep pink velvet pile across Catherine's shoulder. "It must be this, worn with a grey undergown and perhaps a black frontal —" She looked up a little uncertainly. "But perhaps you do not care for it?"

"Your Grace it is unbelievably generous. It is quite lovely but I have served you for such a short time —"

"Then it is decided," the Queen signed to the apprentice to take the bolt of cloth. "A gown length for Lady Kingsford." She put a thin hand pleadingly on Catherine's arm. "Let me have my wish in this, while I have opportunity. Now," she surveyed the shining masses of colour thoughtfully, "ladies, advise me. I would have the King truly proud of me this Christmas. We have been in mourning too long."

Before anyone could make a suggestion the Genoese merchant who had accompanied the two others from the Chepe, snapped his fingers and a youthful apprentice hastened forward to drop on one knee before the Queen while his master busily snipped away at the stitches which kept in place the coarse linen protective cover over a bundle of cloth not yet displayed.

"Allow me, Your Grace." The man's English was good, though heavily accented. "I trust you will be satisfied by the King's gift, the design he specially commissioned for you to wear at the Holy Season."

There was a little gasp of astonishment as the man deftly shook out a shimmering tide of cloth of gold. Picked out in purple thread was the bold design of the Yorkist rose, the heart of each exquisite flower adorned by a tiny seed-pearl. "For the undergown, Your

Grace, and over it, see —" He unfurled, for their bemused gaze, a bolt of rich white velvet which glimmered in the light from the window on a frosting of tiny crystals which adorned the cloth.

Tears sprang to the Queen's eyes as she touched the rich pile with gentle fingers.

"You say the King gave instructions for this design?"

"He did, indeed, Your Grace, but if it does not please you —"

"It does, master merchant," she said softly, "it pleases me well and, of course, I shall wear this for the feasting and no other."

The man nodded, satisfied, and signalled for his apprentice to roll up the precious bolts. The boy was about to do so when the Lady Elizabeth entered the room and stood, blue eyes widening in delight at the unexpected sight of the array of such fine materials. Catherine could well believe that the former Princess had had few opportunities since the death of her father to wear such finery. The gowns she had been wearing recently at Court had revealed signs of wear, despite careful mending.

"Forgive me for my lateness in presenting myself, Your Grace." She sounded a little breathless as if she had been hastening. "Oh, that is truly too fine a sight. It strains the strength of my will. I really must not be envious."

"Bess, how fortunate you came when you did," the Queen welcomed her warmly. "We are all choosing new lengths for the Christmas festivities and naturally you must celebrate with all of us."

"But —"

"Don't spare the cost. The King has given me leave to make presents to all my ladies. He cannot cavil at a gift to my niece and while you are here we must choose for Cecily too and the other girls."

Elizabeth's eyes passed from one bright colour to another.

"They are all so lovely. It is difficult —" She paused and her fingers stole towards the cloth of gold with its design of the rose.

"My father's personal arms. See, the sun burst behind the rose. Oh, Your Grace, may I?"

There was a little awkward silence. The eyes of the ladies avoided those of the Queen and each other's.

Elizabeth felt the sudden change in atmosphere and looked up hurriedly.

"Please, I have said something wrong. My father —"

The Queen gave a little forced laugh. "Of course you have said nothing wrong, Bess. It's natural you should take a fancy to a design so personal to your house. The cloth is the King's gift to me but there is no reason whatever why you should not receive some of it too. Is there sufficient for two gowns, master merchant?"

He blinked rapidly as if not sure how to reply, then nodded unhappily.

"Yes, Your Grace, but —"

"Then see to it. The Lady Elizabeth shall have a length cut from the bolt," then more briskly, "You must take the rest away, masters, or you will tempt us to anger our menfolk by more outrageous extravagances. You have excelled yourselves. Be sure you will have our continued patronage." Her dismissal was gracious and the merchants and apprentices speedily went about the business of furling up the cloths and taking their departure, bowing low.

The Queen summoned a page to play to them, exhorting her ladies afterwards to discuss further the jewels and ribbons they would choose to enhance the materials. The Lady Elizabeth took a stool near the Queen, head bent decorously over an embroidered kerchief she was preparing as a Christmas gift for one member of the family.

Catherine wished with all her heart that she had not caught the look of keen disappointment the Queen had been at some trouble to conceal. What ill fortune had brought the Lady Elizabeth to the Queen's side at such a moment and forced her to share her husband's gift of love with her pretty niece?

Six

Catherine was seated in her own small room the next afternoon busily engaged in sewing the new gown which Maud and she had already cut out. If she was to wear it at Christmas she must take every possible opportunity she could get, since Margery was not available with expert help. She sat very close to the tiny window aperture for the light was already dim in the room and the one brazier seemed to give off little warmth. Maud entered and banged the door shut which startled her. The maid rarely became excited and Catherine had given her permission less than an hour ago to go down to the kitchens in search of Rob. Maud came close as Catherine stifled an exclamation and hastily searched the rose velvet for a marring blood spot.

"Lord, Maud, you caused me to almost jump from my skin. It's fortunate I had no scissors or I might well have ruined the fabric."

Maud bent very low to whisper in her ear. "Can you leave the palace, mistress?"

Catherine's surprise grew. "Yes, I suppose I can, if there's need. The Queen has given me permission to absent myself from her presence for the rest of the day. The King is with her."

"Will you be missed?"

"I doubt it." Catherine's expression was rueful. "My companionship is not sought eagerly by my companion ladies."

"Rob is below. Sir Hugh has given instructions for you to choose a Christmas gift and Rob would like to accompany you into the city."

Catherine shivered and held cold fingers to the brazier of sea coal. "This afternoon? It is very cold, Maud. Tomorrow —"

"You may be needed to wait on the Queen and the opportunity missed."

"Has Rob news from Cadeby?" Catherine's eyes lit up with delight as Maud swathed her in a fur-lined, hooded cloak.

"We'll remove your hennin, mistress. You'll want to put the hood up."

"Do you come with us?"

"I'll continue work on the gown and explain your absence if you are missed."

Catherine laughed. "You are very persuasive. Despite the cold it will be pleasant to be free of the oppressive Court air for a few hours. I must be back by nightfall at the Queen's side when she is ready to retire."

Maud nodded, pulled on her own cloak, tying the strings with impatient fingers clumsy with the cold. "I'll take you to Rob."

The groom was warmly wrapped in frieze cloak and hood and waiting near the King's water steps.

"Mistress, the boat is waiting. Good. I see you are prepared for the journey."

He gave Maud a hurried kiss and helped Catherine into the boat which edged near the steps in readiness.

"Br-rr." Catherine sank back on her seat. As he jumped down the boatman pushed off. "Do you remember? It's almost as cold to-day as on the frosty one I went to Caxton's shop. You stole a boat then. It seems a world away yet only six years."

"Aye, mistress."

She couldn't distinguish his features in the gathering gloom and there was the usual mist over the river.

She had been attacked on her way back to the palace with Queen Elizabeth's gift from her brother, Earl Rivers. Strange to think that elegant scholar dead with his nephew, young Dick Grey, at Pomfret over a year ago. Rob had saved her and conveyed her to the South

Wark where she had remained hidden until Richard's men had found her and, fearing for her safety at the Queen's hands, he had had her conveyed to France in *The Rose of London*.

Rapt in her memories she was startled to discover that the boatman was not making for the bridge as she expected since they were heading for the Chepe. They were now in midstream and clearly making for the South Bank.

"Rob?" She sat up alarmed and scanned the water.

"Hush, mistress," he warned, smiling. "Trust me. I will explain shortly."

Worried though she was, it was her custom to rely on Rob implicitly and when their boat grounded against the far bank and money changed hands, Rob's instructions to their boatman too low for her to catch, she waited as patiently as she could for her groom to re-join her.

This side of the river was the home of the 'Winchester geese' as the harlots who plied their trade in its squalid streets were derisively termed, since the inns and brothels which housed them were owned by the Lord Bishop of Winchester. Catherine's shiver was not entirely due to the cold. She had taken shelter in such a house and even now she could recall vividly the horror of huddling miserably in the garret above while the bawdy jests and rowdy singing went on below and round her.

The streets were almost deserted. Few of the inhabitants of this quarter went about their business until after full dark.

Rob shook his head as she was about to question him, took her hand and led her hurriedly from the water front down a noisome alley to a street of even more dilapidated property whose upper storeys leaned crazily above their heads to almost butt the roofs of those opposite.

He stopped at a corner house and rapped sharply after gazing round as if anxious not to be seen requesting entrance.

The door was half opened and he leaned inwards to whisper his name. At this the door was opened wider and Rob drew Catherine into the evil-smelling interior. The rush dips had not yet been kindled and the oiled parchment panes let little or no light into the place. Catherine's feet slithered on greasy rushes.

"Thanks, Nell," Rob addressed the inhabitant who'd admitted them. As her eyes grew accustomed to the gloom Catherine glimpsed the shape of an enormously fat woman whose frowsty hair, uncovered and dyed almost orange, was oddly familiar. It belonged to a woman who had brought her food in that other house six years ago, a woman whose animal stink had repelled her, yet who had kept her safe from harm or molestation because Rob had willed it so.

Nell chuckled low and though too dark to see clearly Catherine knew how that double chin and flaccid fat cheeks shook with the force of her mirth.

"All's well, Master Rob. You're expected above stairs. I'll kindle the dip lest her ladyship stumble on the stair. Welcome to Nell's humble abode, my lady. You'll not recognize me. It's not to be expected, but it's good to see you safe after these years."

"And good to be able to thank you for your care of me then. You endangered yourself," Catherine said warmly. "How could I help but know you, had it been a lifetime ago and not merely six years."

The woman chuckled again and held up the rush dip to light the stair. Rob went first and, reaching the landing, put down his hand to help her up. In the dimness he retained that steadying hand on her arm while with the other he pushed wide the door of the room which faced them.

"Here she is, safe and sound, sir, and I'll warrant her departure went unnoticed by any at the palace."

He impelled her gently forward, as, with an inarticulate, almost harsh little gasp from the man within, she was pulled into the arms and drawn tight against her husband's breast.

Rob's voice, quiet and respectful, came from the doorway. "I'll be downstairs when you want me, sir."

There was a glint of humour in Hugh's reply. "Behave yourself, man, or Maud will have your hide."

The door was drawn to behind them and Hugh drew Catherine to the window aperture. "Let me look at you."

She took her fill gazing at him, her hands held flat against the leather of his simple jerkin. He was smiling crookedly and looked well but there was a tension in the features, the tightened mouth, the deep groove from the nostrils and the thrust of the chin that told of his hunger for her and something else too, a wariness, somewhat akin to fear. A shiver ran through her.

"Hugh, Hugh, my darling, you should not be here. You are virtually under house arrest at Cadeby. If it is discovered that you —"

Gently he undid her cloak strings, put back the hood and ran a questing hand over her loosened hair.

"You grow more lovely each time I lose you, even for days."

She felt his mouth hard on hers, and hungrily gave way to her own longing, held back for weeks, for the reassurance of his presence.

They drew apart, laughing, almost embarrassed by their own self-conscious betrayal of desire. He leaned out and drew to the weather-beaten window shutters, indicating that she should kindle the rush light in its rusted holder on the rough table.

"How long can you stay?"

"Not long. I must be with Her Grace when she retires."

His hands on her shoulders were urgent, demanding. "Then we must waste no more time."

"You will need to play the maid. These hooks and the sleeve ties are awkward."

He silenced her objections with light kisses on her throat and forehead.

It was more wonderful than she could have dreamed possible. From their marriage night, when she had had no affection, hardly respect for this man, she had gloried in his love-making and her body had played traitor to her heart. Now there *was* love between them, not the heart-stopping passion she felt in the King's nearness, but true affection, sexual desire, an intrinsic understanding and well-placed trust each had for the other.

As she lay in his arms on the sagging rope bed, she felt his body shake with ill-concealed mirth. "Faith, love, it's not the most luxurious love nest. Forgive me. Rob and I disposed of the bedding, so you have little to fear from vermin, but, for all that, I'd have chosen a better place for you, had I dared."

Her fingers lightly traced the loved outline of his facial bones. "Which brings me again to my fear. Hugh, dear heart, you should not have risked this."

"You'd have me go mad with the waiting? Catherine, can I lose you for months without the attempt to hold you in my arms? The risk is slight enough. I came dressed as a mercenary. Rob made the arrangements." She heard him chuckle in the half darkness. "He appears to know this neighbourhood and its denizens amazingly well. We discussed this matter on the very day you left Kingsford."

"The risk is greater than you think," she said soberly. "Colyngbourne is taken and to be arraigned with John Turburvyle at the Guildhall very soon now. The whole atmosphere of the Court is again thick with intrigue and the very stench of fear. You must be careful. How can you know that 'our man'," her voice broke on the words, "was not associated with either or both of them or their masters."

He gave a soft whistle. "Are they now? This certainly makes my presence here more hazardous, for Richard's men-at-arms will be keeping a wary eye on all newcomers to the city and security will be tight."

"If they are found guilty, will they pay the full penalty?"

They had both come so close the full horror of that terror last year that she could hardly frame the words.

"Aye," Hugh said grimly. "Richard can no longer afford to be merciful."

"These men have not raised rebellion on their own accounts. There must be those in high places —" She shivered again. "Be very careful, Hugh. You are known to them. The messenger approached you and now you are understood to be against them, for you repulsed their advances. They will try to trap you. It would be so easy. You have disobeyed the King's orders. Even in May he bade you remain at Kingsford."

She struggled up to sit and look down at him as he lay flat on his back, his head resting on clasped hands. "Tomorrow you must leave the city. Hugh, you must."

His dark eyes glinted in the uncertain flicker of the dip.

"To make a bolt for it now might be more dangerous than to remain in this hole until the trial is over."

She sank back and he gathered her close again to still her trembling.

"Hush, sweet. We are safe provided we take precautions. Forget this ugliness. You have had my messages? The children are well and the baby thrives. Margery and Luce are treasures."

Tears threatened to close up her throat. "I long to hold him in my arms and to have Richard and Janet within my sight. The Queen has promised me leave to come home for Christmas."

"Praise the Virgin. How is the poor lady?"

"Better, for the moment. This last month has not been so foggy or damp as we feared, until to-day. She coughs, but not so badly, and her nights have been more settled."

"What ailed her so badly she needed you?"

"I don't know." Catherine bit her lip in thought. "At least —"

"Yes?"

"I am not sure. She spoke of malicious rumour, gossip."

"Nothing new at Court."

"No."

He sensed something in her constraint and his head shot up and he peered down at her closely.

"You are aware of something which could threaten the King's reputation?"

"No. Yes — oh, I am not sure and if I am wrong —. Hugh, it's the Lady Elizabeth. The King should send her back to her mother, at once."

"The Lady Bessy? Why? Does she intrigue under the noses of Their Graces?"

"No, certainly not. She has a great regard for the King and she dislikes me intensely."

"Why should she?"

"She resents me. They all do, the younger ladies, but she found us in close talk on the day I arrived at Court and I saw something in her eyes, more than curiosity or dislike even, envy, hate? No, I put it too strongly." Catherine plucked awkwardly at the rope supports of the bed beneath her. "Hugh, I believe she is aware that —"

"Your association with the King was not precisely one of dutiful ward and guardian?"

"She *could* not know. No-one did, except Sir Richard Ratcliffe. He was in attendance on Richard that night and — perhaps Lovell suspects. There is little concerning Richard that Francis Lovell does not know. But I do not fear the indiscretion or malice of either of them."

Hugh was silent for a moment then he said, "Are you saying that Lady Bessy's feelings for her uncle are deeper than one might expect to exist between natural affectionate family members?"

"I fear the Queen thinks so and is concerned for the reaction of Richard's friends."

"But he himself is not —"

"He does not know, I am sure he is not even aware of the danger. You know the King, Hugh. Where he loves he lays himself open to all attacks. His kindnesses to Elizabeth Woodville's daughters are exactly what one would expect of him. He is anxious to make up to the girl for the time she was forced to spend so miserably in the Westminster Sanctuary. He plays chess with her, dances, takes her riding and hawking, but people talk. The Queen is known to be ill and the doctors have forbidden him her bed though I can tell you now there are occasions when he defies them. I know all his fears, thoughts, desires, are for Anne." She strove to hide from Hugh her own bitterness. "But she should be from Court, where her fresh prettiness is not daily contrasted with the poor Queen's increasing gauntness, and she should be wed soon to a man Richard can trust." She told him briefly about the morning's incident with the cloth merchants. "I do not believe she could have known, of course, that her choice was the King's gift, yet —"

"Yet you suspect that she contrived it."

"How can I say? I only know that Anne's pleasure was broken immediately the girl made her choice. It was unfortunate, to say the very least. Why isn't she wed? She must be twenty-one. Richard had sworn to make suitable matches for his nieces. He should do so, at once."

Hugh's reply was tempered with faint amusement, as if he read the cause behind the note of asperity in his wife's voice.

"Peace, love. Bess cannot be a threat to the King. Her bastardy declares her of little account in the succession. You say yourself his natural kindness would prevent him from forcing her into a match which might prove abhorrent. Poor lass, it is no fault of hers that the late King's plans to betroth her to the Dauphin came to naught. I imagine Richard is merely allowing her to come to terms with her changed circumstances."

"Yes."

He drew her again into his arms, gently comforting her fears.

When Rob tapped respectfully Hugh made no attempt to detain her, but assisted her into the Court gown, then drew the strings of her cloak close round her throat as he kissed her in parting.

"Rob will inform you if and when it is safe for us to meet again."

She clutched at his sleeve, suddenly more fearful for him. "You will be cautious, not venture into the city?"

"My heart, my love for you prompts me to the utmost care of my hide."

The mist over the river seemed thicker and more menacing as Rob conveyed her back to Westminster. Neither spoke till the King's Steps loomed darkly out of the gloom and their boat jarred against the landing. There were few to note them as they passed through Palace Yard, the inclemency of the weather keeping the palace ladies and courtiers to the proximity of fires and braziers. The guards stamped feet against the cold, shifting miserably, longing for the arrival of their reliefs. Rob met their challenge smoothly and Catherine was soon back in her small room close to the Queen's chamber, where Maud, clucking concern at the mist-damped state of her apparel, hurried to help her change so that she might soon be ready to wait upon the Queen as she was about to retire.

Seven

Catherine went once more to the South Wark one afternoon when the Queen declared herself over-tired and announced her intention of resting throughout the afternoon.

"If Your Grace is unwell, I should summon Dr Hobbes."

"No, really, Catherine. I am pleasantly fatigued. I wish to be fresh for the Christmas festivities and will take the opportunity to rest while I can." She looked shrewdly at her attendant. "I think you are beginning to look somewhat strained, my dear, and would do well today to follow my example."

Catherine curtseyed and withdrew. This was a god-sent opportunity to visit Hugh and she sent Maud to find Rob. Fortunately he was discovered and agreed at once to escort her.

Today there was a cold wind blowing from the north and the air invigorating. The view was clear and she enjoyed the journey down-river in spite of her freezing fingers and toes.

Hugh greeted her joyfully and she could tell he was fretting to be out of doors, not cooped up in the insalubrious attic room. Though she hated to part with him she begged him to leave London.

"Now that Colyngbourne is condemned it is even less safe for you to be here. Hugh, please go. Provided the Queen's health does not deteriorate and I have the King's leave, I shall be home for Christmas."

"Then let me wait and accompany you."

"That would be unwise, Hugh. His Grace may well decide to provide an escort for me."

"Then I stay a few more days in hope of catching one more sight of you."

She relented, sighing, and, since their time together was limited, allowed him to draw her to his heart. It was always a wrench to leave him but she dared not delay and set out again with Rob before two hours were up.

As on the previous occasion she was plainly clad in frieze cloak and hood, so as not to invite notice of her journeying into the city and speculations as to the cause.

As the boatman attempted to hold the small vessel close to the King's Steps at Westminster for her to alight, another boat drew alongside and Catherine recognized the tall form of Lord

Thomas Stanley, as he, too, stepped ashore.

Her attention taken, she almost slipped on the icy cobbles of the quay and, before Rob could come to her aid, Lord Thomas had courteously put out his arm to steady her. She trembled in his grasp and he gave a faint start of recognition.

"Lady Catherine, I had not expected to see you abroad on so raw a day."

She sought frantically for some excuse, thinking he might refer to her journey to the city in conversation with the King, however unwittingly.

"Good even, my lord." She curtseyed and he fell into step beside her, as Rob fell behind respectfully. "It is indeed a dreadfully cold day, though not so damp, for which we are grateful, since the wet worsens Her Grace's cough."

"How is the Queen?"

"Better, my lord, and cheerfully looking to the Christmas festivities."

"You are on an errand for Her Grace?"

"No." To have lied about that would have been dangerously foolish. "I have been to consult an apothecary in the city. Monsieur Chauvet recommended the man."

"I hope I do not find you unwell, Lady Catherine."

She averted her chin as if slightly embarrassed. "Merely indisposed, sir. The apothecary needed to see me, otherwise my maid would have gone."

He nodded, bowed at the entrance to the palace, and went about his business.

Her heart was beating uncomfortably fast as if Lord Stanley had been able to read her guilt and fear for Hugh. She did not like the piercing regard of my lord's cold blue eyes. Nothing, however insignificant, appeared to escape his notice and she had the nervous feeling that he stored away, in that merchant's mind of his, snippets of information and gossip which might prove useful to him in the future. She had not been able to rid herself of the suspicion that it had been Lord Thomas who had brought Lord Lovell's attention to the matter of Hugh's ill-advised letter to the late Lord Hastings.

She liked neither of the Stanley brothers, finding the attentions of the more openly lascivious and impetuous Sir William aggravating, but she feared and distrusted the razor-sharp thought processes of his brother far more. Was he not father-in-law to Henry Tudor, the King's deadliest enemy, and, though he had sworn to the King that he would strictly control all communication between Henry and Lord Thomas's wife, Lady Margaret Beaufort, Catherine could not believe he would keep his word if it suited him to betray his master. Meanwhile the King appeared to court his allegiance, despite that powerful nobleman's former involvement with Lord Hastings and Bishop Morton.

She was thankful to gain the sanctuary of her own small chamber, and, after allowing Maud to attend to her toilet, presented herself in the Queen's apartments for a spell of duty.

Later, after the feasting in the hall, she glimpsed Perron Chauvet elegantly clad as usual in black, a gold chain of superb design swinging from his shoulders. He had been absent from Court since the royal household had settled in Westminster and she had wondered if the man had been about his own concerns or on the King's business.

Deliberately she went to his side. He bowed low with that studied courtesy which unaccountably drew a blush to her cheeks.

"Madame Catherine, my pleasure in your company is as great as ever."

She constantly marvelled at the excellence of his English. On only rare occasions did he break into a French oath, betraying his Burgundian descent.

"I thank you, Monsieur Chauvet." She glanced hurriedly towards the throne dais where Lord Thomas Stanley was in talk with the King. "I have missed you at Court."

He smiled. "I have been to Berkhamstead on an errand from the King to his mother."

Catherine could well believe that there would be communications between Richard and the Duchess Cecily at this time which might require the services of a discreet messenger. William Colyngbourne had been of the Duchess's household and, doubtless, his arrest, trial and condemnation had caused her no little distress.

As if sensing her need Chauvet drew Catherine a little apart, as they walked, making perfunctory conversation concerning the Queen's improved health and Catherine's own duties.

Once free of the press, Catherine placed a confiding hand on the magnificence of his black velvet sleeve.

"Monsier, I require a favour of you."

"Madame, you know I am most happy to oblige you."

"For reasons which I do not wish to disclose, at present," she stumbled out awkwardly, "I was forced to give an excuse to-day to Lord Thomas Stanley for my having been into the city. I regret I mentioned your name, hoping —"

"Tell me, madame, what you wish me to say if I am questioned."

She explained, her cheeks flaming and he nodded gravely.

"Your recent experiences in childbed will prove opportunity for the assumption that you are mildly inconvenienced and not anxious to speak openly of what troubles you. The ruse will serve. I have, indeed, an apothecary who is known to me in Chepeside whose services I call upon frequently to provide me with drugs and herbal infusions."

Relief washed over her. "It is unlikely that any would ask directly but I have my own reasons for not wishing the King to know why I have made two excursions into London and may need to do so again."

"So." Those green eyes danced as they met her own perplexed grey ones. "I am to serve as accomplice. No," he laughed at her sudden alarm, "it pleases me, madame, believe me."

If Catherine had any doubts that Chauvet had understood the dire nature of her need, they were dispelled when he came early to her chamber two days later, even before she had presented herself in attendance. She saw that he was dressed for riding. He glanced back at Maud who had admitted him somewhat unwillingly, his eyebrows raised and Catherine nodded.

"My maid is to be trusted. Rob's wife. What is it, Monsieur?"

He undid his cloak and bent over her chair, placing his two hands on either side of her neck, bending low as if to examine her eyelids for evidence of bloodlessness.

"Is Sir Hugh in the city?"

She quivered under his hold, alarm widening her grey eyes.

"If he is, he could be in grave danger to-day. Colyngbourne is to suffer on Tower Hill to-day at noon and the King's men will take up positions wherever crowds gather and at the city gates."

"The gates, why?"

"The King's advisers have warned him of some sympathetic to the man's cause and there are always those who attend such spectacles, either to deliberately fan insurrection or, excited by the blood-lust, turn to violence mindlessly."

"But surely there will be no search of houses."

"Not impossible." The word was spoken under stress in the French intonation. "If there is any kind of trouble, Sir Hugh is best out of the city before violence erupts."

"I must go, warn him."

"Madame Catherine, you will trust me?"

She hesitated only briefly then nodded.

"Your groom can instruct him where to meet me."

"But why? Would he not be wiser to leave straightaway?"

"He may not be passed through the gate. I ride north on the King's business. I am to take the apothecary's son, the man of whom I spoke. Dressed in such garments Sir Hugh could leave with me under the King's seal before he could be inadvertently embroiled in any upsurge of hysteria."

"The Virgin bless you." They were whispering close, mouth to ear, as pages listened at every door in the close confines of the Court. "But I must go with you."

He shook his head gently. "Not advisable."

"But he may refuse to go. I can make him. He must." It was a wail of despair.

"Madame, it would be unsafe for you to venture into London to-day."

"I dressed as a page once, as a child. I could do it again."

His mocking gaze passed over her. "Madame Catherine, I fear such an adventure would be unlikely to prove successful now."

"Then I could go dressed as Maud. We exchanged roles once before. I could plead sickness and she remain in my bed to cover my absence. Please, Monsieur Chauvet, you need me to convince Hugh of his danger."

He considered then nodded. "Call the

woman and explain. We must make haste. In her guise you will accompany me to the apothecary in Chepeside for a remedy for 'your mistress'. *Mordieu*, I am not happy at this, but, *vraiment*, if I must, I must."

Rob made only a grunt of assent when Maud led him into Catherine's room, where, already, she was cloaked and hooded in Maud's garments.

"I can bring Sir Hugh to the Chepe, sir." His gaze flickered to Catherine and he frowned.

"Please Rob, I insist on seeing him," she said before he could object.

"The city will be crowded with undesirables."

"We know that, man," Chauvet said irritably. "Your mistress will go directly to the apothecary with me from the bridge landing steps. I am expected, though the shop will be barred and shuttered, in expectation of looting."

Maud hastily donned Catherine's night shift while the men looked away.

"I have already mentioned your illness to Lady Isobel's maid," she said quietly. "I think you will not be disturbed. She knows I go into the city for a potion to ease your pain."

Catherine touched the woman's arm gratefully. "I shall hurry back with Rob." She shuddered. "I've no wish to linger near the Tower to-day."

It did not prove as easy as Chauvet had thought to head for their destination when Catherine and her escorts landed at London Bridge. As they attempted to move from Dowgate towards Cornhill and the entrance to Chepeside they were met by a solid mass of citizens intent on seeing the bloody spectacle soon to be enacted at Tower Hill. Crushed between the two men, Catherine almost panicked. Already many of the apprentices and townsfolk were drunk and in no mood to give ground. The cobbles beneath her feet were greasy with spilt ale, wine and vomit. She drew a hard breath lest she herself fall sick, nauseated by the rank stench of humanity and its avid desire to view the barbarity the law demanded for convicted traitors.

Chauvet bellowed in Rob's ear. "You must get back to the bridge."

"I'd have the mistress safe bestowed first, sir. The master —"

"Get back, man, before the crowd boxes us in completely. Wait until this is over before coming to Chepeside. You cannot miss the shop. The apothecary's sign is displayed, the only one with a huge red retort above the door."

Immediately the seething mass closed round

Rob and he was lost to view.

Chauvet bent close. "Hold tight to my arm, madame. We must go along with the crowd. It is useless to attempt to go against the stream till later."

Catherine was terrified. The good-humoured bantering of the normally decent men and women around her was unbelievable. Dear God, did no-one consider the coming suffering of the condemned prisoner? Surely there must be some among the sightseers sympathetic to his cause, many, indeed, who had found his wit highly entertaining. Already he would be thought to be paying this terrible price because he had ridiculed his King, rather than the bitter truth, that he was indeed a traitor and had been found guilty of trying to persuade one Yate, to join Henry Tudor in Brittany. Though there was little to excuse Colyngbourne's actions, considering he had been a trusted servant of the Duchess of York, she could not forbear to pity him now. She recalled her husband's confession of heart-stirring fear in Warwick Castle, and her lips moved in prayer to the gentle Virgin that the man might die speedily while the hangman did his dread work with the rope and before the commencement of the butchery that would turn a living man's body into the bloody carcase of shambles meat.

Neither she nor the prisoner was to be spared anything.

Relentlessly she and Chauvet were pushed to Tower Hill. They were good-humouredly edged towards the scaffold site, despite Chauvet's pleas to 'let the woman through'. These were either ignored or countered with a bawdy encouragement to 'go, view the proceedings'.

He held her tight pressed against his body. "We must stay here with our backs to this wall until these distasteful proceedings are over, madame. Try not to look. I will get you free the moment I can."

She turned her face against the rough weave of his cloak in an attempt to shut out the shouting, gesticulating mob which hemmed them in, but the new gallows was built high and her gaze was inevitably drawn to the sight of the middle-aged, thin-looking man who climbed the ladder, seemingly willingly enough, and in a bewildered fashion, as if he could not believe himself to be really in such a dire situation. Witticisms were hurled at him as well as shameful exhortations to the executioner who stood, stolid and brawny, clad in the black garments and leathern apron of his trade.

Shudderingly Catherine recalled another occasion when she had seen a man die, her father, but quickly and with dignity.

This death was to be neither. She averted her eyes when the noose was adjusted and the roar of the watchful crowd mounted to a frenzy. She caught an unavoidable glimpse of the executioner and his assistant throw their victim down onto a prepared, wooden table, choked on the scream of raucous delight which met the castration. Bile rose in her throat. Sweet Virgin, those were women's voices! She was hardly aware of Chauvet's efforts to comfort her. Colyngbourne said something she was unable to catch, for the crowd fell suddenly silent, then there was the horrifying stink of burning flesh.

Then and only then was Chauvet able to draw the half-fainting woman free of the press. He beat aside impatiently those who came on, anxious to gloat on what yet remained to be done of the quartering and, lifting Catherine to his shoulder, carried her the rest of the way to the shop in the Chepe.

An elderly housewife shouted a gruff comment that "Women who couldn't bear such sights should stay at home in future and tend the house."

"Madame, *ma pauvre petite,* we are here at least," he said as he gently set her down.

The rear door was unbarred and an elderly man, thin and stooping, ushered them inside.

"Master Fowler, I am afraid this lady is grossly unwell."

"In here, Monsieur, lay her on the settle."

Catherine felt herself laid down on the hard wooden bench and something soft placed behind her head. Chauvet moved away and she found herself crying weakly. When he returned he carried a bowl which exuded a faintly aromatic scent. He proceeded to loosen her wimple and bathe forehead and hands. The apothecary waited quietly at his side with a fair linen napkin. Beyond him, in the doorway to the solar, Catherine was aware of a younger man, but his face was in shadow.

Chauvet explained. "We were unable to move clear of the crowd bound for the execution and found ourselves forced to the scaffold site."

"Then the lady saw —"

"Some of it, unfortunately. There is a certain fascination. One finds it hard to avoid looking," Chauvet said dryly.

The older apothecary crossed himself. "Praise God the man's sufferings are over. We live in a violent age, Monsieur."

"If all we hear of the past is true, when has there not been such an age?" The younger man now stepped into the room. Like his father, for Catherine saw he resembled the old man, he wore the dark gaberdine of his calling.

He held out a cup to her.

"Drink, mistress. If you feel sick and faint the posset will help."

The liquid was bitter but not unpleasant. As he predicted it appeased the burning sickness she was fighting to hold back.

"Thank you, sirs." She glanced gratefully at the young apothecary. "I am a coward. I knew what had to be faced but my woman's heart rebelled at the reality."

"Not to be wondered at." The young man's eyes smouldered. "Such practices are an affront to God and the Gentle Saviour."

His father cast him a faintly apprehensive and warning glance.

"The King has been merciful in the past, Arthur. The man is a self-avowed traitor. To show mercy is judged weakness, the more is the pity."

His son sighed. "You may well be right, my father, for those of us who live in the city and remained away from the spectacle are few enough, the saints know."

He turned to Chauvet, "When you are ready for me, sir, call. I'll be above stairs."

"One moment." Chauvet recalled him. "Can I trust you to assist this lady?"

The man turned hastily, looked down at Catherine and inclined his head. "Certainly."

"Even if in the work there lies an element

of danger, remembering well the butchery from which we have just come?"

The man swallowed. Catherine saw his Adam's apple move convulsively. "Even so."

"Then will you and your father come apart with me while I explain what has to be done? The lady waits for someone she holds dear. She will recover now." He smiled at Catherine encouragingly. "I have never known her to lack courage."

She forced herself to rise and move around the room. To lie and think just now would prove unbearable. If Hugh were to be accused, further implicated by sly insinuation, he could suffer that ghastly fate, pulled to the scaffold on a hurdle, half hanged, castrated and his bowels ripped from his living body, as had the man she had just seen die before her eyes.

Where was Hugh now? Had Rob managed to reach him? Surely Hugh would not have been foolish enough to venture into the city to test for himself the mettle of Richard's security?

The room was expensively furnished and scrupulously clean. Like many merchants and professional men Master Fowler was clearly prosperous. She wondered, fleetingly, if like others of his profession he catered for more dubious clients who required love philtres and poisons. She thought not. The kindliness and dignity of the old man had impressed her. But why had Perron Chauvet the need of this man's services, so essential to his work in the north? Master Fowler, the son, was to accompany him so it must be to treat some patient. Yet the King's son was dead. Did the youthful Earl of Warwick require skilled medical attention? Both the King's natural son, John, and his nephew, John of Lincoln, were known to be healthy and lusty, certainly so in the case of the latter whose reputation caused delighted mirth among the younger of the Queen's ladies. Catherine moved restlessly over the finely woven carpet to the doorway of the shadowed shop, wisely shuttered today, against the possibility of looting from an excited populace.

She saw dimly, in the gloom, shelves bearing phials, bottles, boxes of herbs, the whole permeated by an aromatic, scented, not unpleasant odour, reminiscent of her still-room at Kingsford. Had she been less anxious she would have found the place enthralling, for, since her days assisting the infirmarian at Tewkesbury, she had retained her interest and enthusiasm for the compiling of herbs into healing potions and salves.

Chauvet descended the stair and she turned to him anxiously.

"Will he do it?"

"Yes. He leaves the city immediately and will meet us at Barnet. One of his robes should fit Sir Hugh tolerably well."

She paced from settle to fireplace. "Why doesn't he come?"

"Rob will have experienced similar difficulties to our own."

She shuddered. "Monsieur Chauvet, did — did you hear what the prisoner said?"

"Colyngbourne?"

"At the end when —"

"Something about 'more trouble' and called upon Jesus."

"Dear God, that he should still feel —"

"Do not trouble your gentle heart further, Madame Catherine. He —"

She turned on him savagely. "You do not know me, Monsieur Chauvet. My 'gentle heart' cursed men to their ruin and death when I was a child. I would willingly condemn this traitor if he sought to harm the King's Grace, but this — this unspeakable barbarity — and that it could touch Hugh —"

Chauvet's green eyes gleamed in the firelight. She felt he was restraining an urge to come to her, touch her, and that his indolent pose on his stool covered desires he would not unleash.

Both of them started abruptly as urgent blows sounded on the rear door of Master

Fowler's premises.

Chauvet prevented Catherine from rushing into the passage. "Wait, let Master Fowler attend to it. This may be a customer. If so, we do not wish to have gossip concerning your presence here."

There was a mutter of talk after the drawing of the heavy bolts, then quick steps along the passage and she was held in Hugh's arms, crying and laughing hysterically in her joy and relief.

"Steady, my love, steady." He put her gently from him at last and turned to Perron Chauvet. "It seems I am to be in your debt, Monsieur."

"If you will trust your person to me, sir."

Catherine clawed at Hugh's arm. "You must go. Dear God, if you had seen what I have this day —"

He turned, tight-lipped, to Chauvet but any remonstrance from him was forestalled.

"It could not be prevented. The crowd forced us to Tower Hill and, I think you know, Sir Hugh, why she is here."

Hugh sighed, reaching out to clasp Catherine's fingers gently. "I know well, but you too must return to Westminster the moment Rob returns, Dear Heart."

"Where is he?" Her alarm returned.

Hugh gave a grim smile. "Occupied on business of his own, I fear, but I trust to Rob to take care of himself — and others, if necessary." As Catherine's face whitened further he explained. "He was convinced that he had been followed from the palace."

"But Hugh, how could that be possible?"

"Very possible, my love. Every gentleman in service in the household has spies to observe the coming and going of every other gentleman or that officer's retainers."

"But Rob said nothing to me."

"He had no wish to alarm you. Naturally he had thrown off pursuit by the time he reached me at the brothel, but he thought it advisable for him to draw off the fellow further, slip into a cloak of mine and go out again, allowing me to leave later in another direction, just in case. He will come back for you the moment he thinks it safe to do so." He frowned. "I would rather stay here, Monsieur Chauvet, and see that he *does* return safely to provide my wife with an escort back to Westminster."

Chauvet shook his head decisively. "Out of the question, Sir Hugh, we must be out of the city gate while there is some confusion. Please go above stairs where garments are laid out for your use." He put up a hand to check Hugh's objection. "Master Fowler will accompany Madame Catherine to Westminster if need be."

Catherine's eyes implored Hugh to obey. He gave a stiff half-bow and went.

"Will Rob be safe?" She framed the question in a whisper, knowing she could receive only Chauvet's familiar shrug in answer.

"He seems, how do you English say it, — resourceful?"

She gave a nervous little laugh. If Rob saw the need to protect his own he would kill without mercy, but more corpses to dispose of could only give rise to more suspicion.

When Hugh returned his tall form was clothed in the grey-blue gaberdine of the apothecary and he wore the black hood of the profession. He looked older than his years. Chauvet nodded approvingly.

"This will serve, and now, sir, I will leave you one moment with your lady, then we must go."

Catherine clung to Hugh wordlessly. He tilted back her chin in its unfamiliar wimple, smiling at her fear.

"There have been days when I have been tempted to journey to Westminster and throw myself on the King's mercy."

"No — Hugh —."

"Why should I skulk in hiding as if I had committed some crime?"

"Not now — while the shadow of Colyngbourne's treason envelopes the city like a black pall."

"Aye, I have too much to lose, and there is the boy. I would not have you lose him, if the King is angered by further actions of mine. God guard you, my wife." He kissed her soundly then she released him with a little push in the direction of the door. Chauvet paused momentarily in the entrance and she quelled her fears to wish him 'godspeed'.

"My gratitude —"

"Madame, my every wish is to serve you."

"If you should lose by this — of the King's favour."

A ghost of a smile played round those finely cast lips. "I shall not, Madame Catherine, that I promise."

She heard the rear door close quietly on their departure and set herself, with what patience she could summon, to await Rob's return and the long days before she could be certain Hugh was safe. Master Fowler came to her side, soft-footed, solicitous.

"You will eat, mistress. You will need all your strength."

She smiled her thanks and agreed, to please him, then seated herself on the oak settle as noise in the street from the shop front told her citizens were returning to their properties. If Rob were delayed she would be compromised by a failure to wait on Her Grace later, unless Maud's plea of indisposition could serve to keep her undisturbed in their chamber.

Rob returned an hour later. He looked grim but triumphant. As Master Fowler was present she forbore to question him, only too relieved to see him unharmed. Gravely she thanked the apothecary for his kindness and courtesy.

"You had best take this with you." He offered her a glass container. She looked from the dark red liquid to his smiling features.

"The potion is pleasant-tasting and completely harmless in case you are forced to swallow some of it in front of witnesses."

She laughed. "Oh, I had forgotten my ruse for coming into the city. Thank you, again, Master Fowler. You will inform me when —"

"As soon as I have word I will send my apprentice to the palace."

Rob hurried her to the bridge quay. Straggling groups were making their way from taverns and ale-houses in the direction of Tower Hill. It seemed to Catherine that many individuals seemed unwilling to catch her eye, and bore an ill-at-ease, haunted expression as if now that their bloodlust was sated they were ashamed of their lapse into barbarity.

"Rob, you were not forced to kill."

"Nay, mistress," he grinned, leaning on his

oars, for he had indeed been forced to "borrow" the vessel as he put it, no boatman having been available, "our friend will reach his master safely enough and report that I spent a pleasant afternoon in a brothel while my wife was delayed at the apothecary's shop. I'll be certain to boast of my prowess this evening."

"He made no attempt to accost you in Sir Hugh's garments?"

"None. He appeared more interested in my movements, as I suspected. I led him a fine chase, stopped in an alehouse and returned to Nell's." He yelped with laughter, "When I emerged in my own livery he followed. I dodged him and stole a boat. God knows when he managed to cross. The bridge has been packed tight with sightseers the whole day, so I doubt if he has picked up our trail."

"Rob, the bridge crossing is dangerous."

"Only at high tide when the currents are fierce under the supports."

She could not prevent a bubble of laughter herself in spite of the gravity of their situation.

"The boatman will find this simply enough floating down river. He will believe, in his careless haste to view the spectacle of the day, he did not tie it securely to the moorings."

Muffling herself in Maud's cloak against the cold she found it a simple matter to regain her chamber. Maud sat up, relieved, throwing back the covers of the bed.

"Rob is safe and so, thank the Virgin, I think is Sir Hugh. Have you been disturbed here?"

"Lady Isobel knocked and I replied rather faintly. She did not enter. I think you should take to your bed now, mistress. I will report to the Queen's ladies that you are still considerably unwell and unable to perform your duties tonight. It would look better than if you appear to recover too soon."

"Certainly." Catherine nodded as Maud helped her to undress and swiftly don a night shift. She had hardly made herself comfortable, when an imperious knock sounded at the door. Maud eyed her, frightened, and Catherine gestured her to the door now that she had put on the garments her mistress had discarded.

"See who it is. Make some excuse if you can. Leave that phial on the chest near me."

In seconds, after a whispered consultation, Maud sped to the bed, her eyes wide with alarm.

"It is the King's Grace."

"Admit him."

He stood in the doorway, the light flickering coldly on the cabochon cut emeralds in his chain.

"They told me you are ill."

Joy mingled with guilty fear in her tangled

emotions. He concerned himself still with her welfare. She struggled up in the bed.

"Forgive me, Your Grace —"

"Don't try to get up. Rest. Have you consulted Hobbes? I'll see that he comes quickly."

"No, sir, that will not be necessary. You are considerate as ever, but Monsieur Chauvet prescribed medicine which appears to be helpful." She indicated the potion, inwardly thanking Master Fowler's good sense in reminding her to bring it. "Unfortunately I ran out of it after my last visit to the apothecary. My maid has been but delayed —" Her voice trailed off, uncertainly.

His lips tightened in the expression she knew well.

"Unfortunate she found it necessary, today, of all days."

"Yes." She whispered the words, finding it hard to meet his eyes.

"You look very pale, Catherine."

"I have lost blood heavily, Your Grace. It is nothing serious, a woman's problem since the birth of my child."

"And Chauvet is convinced you will soon recover?"

"Oh, yes."

"You must go home tomorrow and rest for a while, if you can travel. I'll order a litter."

"Your Grace is kind but —"

"I insist. I'll not have your illness on my conscience. There is enough on that already."

It was harshly spoken and her heart bled for him. He had not been present near that gallows but she guessed he had imagined every pang of the dying man. Her hand stole to his scarlet velvet sleeve.

"It was necessary."

"Yes, so my advisers insisted — but the man had served my family."

"I know."

"Trubevyle was not so seriously implicated. He shall stay under close guard for a while but Colyngbourne —" His voice broke off. "But we must not speak of this further. Hugh will be thankful to see you after these long weeks." He bent and gave her a guardian's cool kiss upon her cheek. "You would tell me if there was real cause for alarm about your condition?"

"I swear it."

He stood up, moving to the door in a swish of velvet stiff with embroidery.

"If you are well you will return to us by Twelfth Night? We shall be feasting royally and I would have you spend the last day of the Christmas festivities with us."

She nodded, bowing her head to hide her expression. Had that royal 'us' included the

Queen or was he making it clear to her that he would personally feel her absence from Court for the rest of the Holy Season?

Eight

It was delightful to be at Kingsford again. Here
one could be free to speak and move without
fear of prying eyes catching a weakness or indiscretion. The children were overjoyed to see
her and it was wonderfully satisfying to sit
near the fire in the hall with Wilfred content
upon her lap. Bless him, he was gaining weight
steadily and a happy baby. Cecily came to
them from Tewkesbury and Janet was in a
ferment of delight when Catherine told her
the Queen's parting words.

"Bring Janet back with you, Catherine. She
will enjoy the Twelfth Night feasting and will
be company for you. Is it not time for her
to try her wings in Court circles? Will Hugh
object?"

He had not. That first time he had seen
her step from the litter he had been strangely
silent, as if he could not believe she had truly
arrived. Only later, in the privacy of their bedchamber, he had caressed her so fiercely she

thought her ribs would crack.

"Did you have trouble?" she asked at last. "Is Chauvet safe on his way?"

"We were not even questioned when he produced the King's seal, though every conveyance was searched and the men-at arms were sizing up all who were pushing through Moorgate. Some were being detained. It was well I was not asked to prove my identity. Chauvet should be in York or farther north by now. We travelled to Stamford together. The young apothecary joined us at Barnet."

"Did Chauvet give a reason for his journey?"

Hugh shot her an odd glance.

"No, and I did not ask. I gathered one of the royal children required attention."

"Young Warwick?"

"Perhaps." He changed the subject abruptly. Neither of them was confident enough to put thoughts into words. Were Edward's sons safe in the north, and did Chauvet's hasty ride there concern the health of one of them?

The weather continued cold but fresh over Christmas and Catherine was pleased that it had not snowed when she set out south on the last day of December so she would be present at Court for Epiphany as the King had requested. This time an excited Janet accompanied her with Rob and Maud still in attendance.

She found that a larger chamber had been put at her disposal to accommodate Janet and there was a second one for Maud which, doubtless, Rob would share. This courtesy was unprecedented for the palace was packed to overflowing and Isobel Winton confided to Catherine in an unguarded moment that there had been much to-ing and fro-ing of the King's commissioners throughout the festivities.

"It is my belief that His Grace is not satisfied that invasion is ruled out of possibility even at this season," she said, sinking her voice and glancing hurriedly round to see they were not overheard.

"The King is right to take precautions for the safety of the Realm," Catherine reminded her wearily, but her heart sank. Could not Richard have some respite, even at this blessed time?

The Queen's ladies received her more warmly than she had expected. Mary Winton informed her, frowning, "It has rained these last days and Her Grace is troubled again by her cough which has sorely disturbed her rest, and, since she has not retired early one night in a row since Christmas Eve, she needs every hour of sleep she can get."

Hastily Catherine attended Anne, presenting Janet. As Mary had said, the Queen looked tired, hollow-eyed, and Catherine misliked the flush of red which dyed the accented cheek bones, but she greeted them warmly, graciously bade Janet sit close to her while she questioned her about Kingsford and the younger children.

The Christmas feasting was coming to its close with tonight's banquet, and the choice of gowns and jewellery was foremost in the conversation of the Queen's ladies.

Catherine had worn the rose velvet gown, the Queen's gift, once, on Christmas Day that Hugh and the children could admire her finery. Now she donned it again over its grey silk undergown and smoothed back her thick, fair hair beneath the truncated hennin beaded in silver over black velvet while Maud deftly arranged the yards of silk veiling to her satisfaction.

Janet was in her yellow gown and her fresh, dark loveliness was not lost on the pages and younger gentlemen of the King's household when she made her entrance in the Queen's train.

Both Anne and Richard were splendidly clad for the occasion, the King in scarlet and cloth of gold and unaccustomedly regal in his crown and furred mantle, the Queen in her newest gown cut from his splendid gift, the glittering white velvet with its droplets of crystal held high over the magnificence of the cloth of gold and purple underskirt with its design of the Yorkist Rose. Her fair hair hung loose to her shoulders, and it was still glorious enough to vie with the gold of her crown. There was a little gasp of admiration as the royal pair took their place under the Cloth of Estate at the head of the table. To-night the King's mother, the Duchess Cecily, was present and Catherine curiously eyed the Dowager Queen a little subdued in a gown of mauve velvet.

It was a joyful gathering. If the Queen had become over-fatigued she did not betray it as she graciously seconded the King's words of welcome to their guests. The laughing and delighted banter was hushed momentarily as the Lady Elizabeth was announced. Catherine, watching, saw every trace of colour drain from the Queen's face, even to her lips, at the sight of the girl. The former princess's gown was almost identical to the Queen's. She had even chosen to wear her own hair loose under a simple coronet. There was an uncomfortable gap in the proceedings as the Lady Elizabeth advanced and knelt before the Throne dais. Graciously Richard raised her and gave her the kiss of greeting but there was a chill note in his voice and Catherine judged that for once he was not entirely pleased with his niece. Throughout the meal Catherine picked at the richly spiced meats and the subtleties. Her mind was on the disappointed Queen's awareness that Elizabeth's youthful appearance in the costly gown had quite outshone her own presence, shadowing her in her husband's eyes. Why hadn't the girl the sense to discover when the Queen intended to wear it, and what design she had chosen or had she deliberately discovered the truth and decided to flaunt her beauty before the woman she considered her rival?

A little tired after her journey and perplexed by the latest turn of events, Catherine paid little heed to the boisterous proceedings. Janet, flushed with delight, danced many times. Catherine noted that the Queen did not do so. Lord Lovell and Sir Richard Ratcliffe both invited Catherine onto the floor, enquiring politely about Hugh and the situation at Kingsford. Catherine saw Lovell's tight-lipped glance of annoyance as the King danced with his niece. She had expected the Queen to retire early to-night but she remained by her husband's side throughout, even though Catherine believed she was longing to leave the hall and seek her bed.

At last the ladies were summoned and the

Queen took her departure.

As she entered her suite she stumbled and would have fallen had not Catherine caught at her arm.

"Dear lady, you should have been in your bed this last hour," she chided gently.

"I could not break up the mirthful proceedings. We have had little occasion to rejoice this past year."

Wearily she allowed Catherine and Mary Winton to divest her of her state garments, donned her shift and furred bedgown and sat in her chair near the fire while Catherine brought her mulled wine.

"You have eaten little. I was watching. This will help you to sleep."

The Queen took the cup and sipped, then suddenly fell to a bad bout of coughing. Catherine took back the cup and waved away the other ladies.

"Give her air."

Anne gave a frightened cry, a bubbling gasp and choked for breath, catching blindly for a linen napkin Catherine was holding ready for her to dab her lips after taking the wine. Mary Winton uttered a startled scream as the white linen against the Queen's mouth was stained with bright blood. Frantically the Queen held it there but she was terrified and Catherine hastily took charge.

"Mary, help me to get Her Grace to bed. One of you, summon Dr Hobbes. The rest leave us, and do not chatter."

Mary smothered her rising panic and rushed to obey.

"Pillows," Catherine commanded, "Her Grace must sit high."

Gently she smoothed back the Queen's bright hair. "Take comfort, madam, the bout is subsiding. Breathe slowly, steadily. Try not to cough."

The bed sheets and night shift were already marked with crimson, slimy to the touch, and, knowing Mary's horror, she drew the bed curtains close round the Queen and pulled the girl to the door.

"Fetch His Grace. Tell him the Queen has been taken ill, nothing of this bleeding. You understand?" Her fingers dug cruelly into the girl's shoulders in an effort to force some measure of control and she gave her a final, urgent, little shake. "You must not over-alarm those gentlemen with His Grace."

Mary gave a half-frightened nod and hurried off. Catherine returned to her charge.

The worst of the bout was over, but Anne was still choking and coughing. She looked bloodless and her eyes appealed to Catherine over the fresh napkin she held to her lips.

"The King, do not tell him. I have been

at pains — to — to keep these attacks from him."

"Do not talk, Your Grace. Sit very still. He must be told. I would be failing in my duty if I did not inform him."

"If I die —"

"Your Grace is not about to die." Catherine spoke with confidence she did not feel. She was relieved when the door of the bed-chamber opened and the King hastened in. Obviously he had been in bed or about to retire as he was in his bedgown.

"Anne, my darling." His eyes took in the state of the bed and Catherine saw them register horror but he sat on the bed and took his wife's thin hand in his own, squeezing it gently. "Rest still now. There is nothing to fear. Has Hobbes been sent for?"

"Yes, Your Grace."

"I began to cough. It has happened before but — never so badly."

The King shook his head at the Queen's effort to speak as it caused her to cough again weakly. "Foolish one, do not try to talk."

The doctor arrived and took charge, approving Catherine's action in supporting the Queen's shoulders, seating her high. He forbade her to talk and set about preparing a draught which would soothe and ease the cough. Catherine waited to take the cup to the Queen. The old man shot her a searching glance under beetling brows.

"It's bad. You know that?"

"Yes — should, should we summon her confessor?"

He pursed his lips. "I think not. Not that bad, praise the saints — yet." He sighed heavily, "I dread the task of explaining to His Grace."

"I think the King knows how gravely ill she is, Master Hobbes."

"She must stay in her bed now —"

"I understand."

Richard stayed with his Queen till she lay back exhausted, but fear of further haemorrhaging seemed unlikely. At last she slept under the influence of warmed milk laced with powdered poppy seed. Catherine kept watch, rising only once to go to the outer chamber when Mary Winton summoned her timidly.

"It is the Lady Elizabeth. She has heard —"

Catherine's eyes blazed fury. "I gave instructions to those foolish women to guard their tongues."

Elizabeth was still wearing the white velvet gown. Catherine's anger melted when she saw how concerned she was.

"I hear Her Grace has haemorrhaged. Lady Catherine, she is not like to —"

"Die? No, my lady. It has been a bad bout but she should recover with rest and care." She did not need to add the unspoken thoughts, 'This time.'

"This feasting has been too much for her."

Catherine's grey eyes met those Plantagenet blue ones. "Undoubtedly recent events have proved to bring about this collapse."

The Lady Elizabeth dropped her gaze.

"Is there anything I can do?"

"I shall stay with her throughout the night. She will need to be kept very quiet over the next few days but she is always pleased by your presence."

The Queen's cough seemed better in the morning but she was utterly exhausted and kept to her bed for the next week. Soon she was insisting upon rising, though her doctors advised bed rest. Throughout the next weeks Catherine was able to spend little time with Janet and was relieved that Mary Winton appeared to have taken to her and that the girl was not so lonely at Court. Letters came frequently from Hugh. She knew he fevered for her return to Kingsford but, as the Queen's condition worsened, she knew that to be impossible.

Anne struggled on valiantly giving the appearance of normality but by the middle of February was forced to once more take to her bed. Catherine recognized instinctively that she would not again rise from it. Both Lady Elizabeth and Clarence's daughter, Lady Margaret, were constantly at the Queen's side, reading to her, relating the gossip of the Court. Richard came to her chamber daily and sent messengers to enquire about her condition whenever he was delayed in Council. Perron Chauvet arrived from the north and it did not need his sober countenance to tell Catherine that the end was very near.

On a cold but sunny morning in March the Queen appeared to rally. She seemed stronger when the King made his morning visit, the pale light touching fresh colour in her cheeks. Catherine was touched by his pleasure in her improvement. She had had a restful night and smilingly bade him hasten to a meeting of the Council at the Tower.

Catherine was busied in sorting through the Queen's gowns for protection during the coming season when damage from moths would occur when Isobel, white-faced, summoned her to the bedside. The Queen had haemorrhaged again, badly.

Afterwards, when Dr Hobbes and Chauvet had left, having made her as comfortable as they could, shaking their heads and murmuring that the Queen's confessor be called and His Grace informed of the gravity of her condition, Catherine came to sit by the bed at her request. Anne's hand stole out and seized her own.

"I said, you will remember, that I would not speak to you of this again — until it was time."

Catherine fought against the weight of unshed tears which threatened to choke her. "Dear madam —"

"You know that time is now, as I do. That is why I have sent them all away. You will comfort him, Catherine? You will know how to find the words." She looked away, whispering, "I think you are aware of the danger to him which I fear."

"Yes, Your Grace."

"He must be counselled by his friends, do nothing to bring him into the disrepute of those who love him, particularly the men of the north. Later, he must be made to marry again — and soon." The last words were fiercely spoken. "I have been too long dying, Catherine, holding him back from siring an heir."

"Madam —"

Anne's hand silenced her with a tightening grip on her wrist. There was noise behind them. The Queen's confessor entered hurriedly and Catherine rose to allow him to approach the bed but the Queen's hand imperatively held her back for one second.

"Guard your sons, Catherine. Kiss them for me. I would have wished to see them."

The King came, bewildered, from the Tower, like a man injured from some grave blow and unable to comprehend how he came by it. Catherine stood with the Queen's women while she received Extreme Unction. The room filled and there was a blur of candle flame and the gleam of sunlight on cross and pyx, the heavy scent of incense and the muted sound of chant and prayers. Richard sat on a stool holding the dying Queen in his arms. She looked like a tired child.

Then he dismissed them all.

Dr Hobbes shot an anxious glance an hour later at Catherine as she waited quietly near the door of the Queen's chamber. She shook her head in answer to his silent enquiry, then he went in and Catherine heard the murmur of voices.

When Richard emerged with him he walked stiffly as if in armour.

"You must leave Her Grace to her ladies now, sir." Hobbes was very gentle, signalling to Catherine that it was over. The King went with him unresisting, till Lord Lovell hastened forward to escort him to his own apartments. As she rose from the stool to enter the chamber Catherine was aware of the soft, hopeless weeping of the Queen's ladies behind her in the antechamber. It was March sixteenth.

She walked with the Queen's ladies in the solemn funeral *cortège* to the Abbey, averting her eyes from their avid curiosity as the King wept unashamed.

There was no reason now to delay her departure from Westminster, so she went about her preparations methodically, yet she was unable to leave Court without the King's express permission, and he kept to his apartments, giving no audiences. Her position of isolation appeared now to have increased, since she had nothing in common with the other ladies. Her inability to comfort the King lay like a heavy weight on her heart.

The noise of the Court which had so irritated herself and Maud was now unnaturally hushed. Officials moved by garbed in sober black, their expressions grave, while others drew together to whisper in groups, turning heads hurriedly and breaking off talk abruptly as others passed close and might overhear them.

She wrote to Hugh giving him the details she knew he would wish to know, having had deep affection over the years for the frail and gentle Queen, since he had served her father, Great Warwick, as page and squire.

Now she had time to give to Janet it seemed

no occasion for them to view the city or frequent the shops of Chepeside. The girl would chatter to her brightly then break off as if ashamed of her own selfish assumption that all was well. It would be hard for Janet to return now to Leicestershire as she appeared to have made friendships at Court, yet she made no comments regretting Catherine's intention to leave soon for home.

When at last Catherine was able to approach Lord Lovell with her request to return to Kingsford, he looked at her keenly.

"I would deem it a favour, Lady Catherine, if you would delay for a little longer."

"The King is disinclined to grant my request?"

"I have not yet importuned him with anything but the most pressing affairs. He has shut himself from everyone. It was to be expected. The boy, John, waits upon him now. Thank God the lad is sensible and discreet."

"I understand."

How could she leave without seeing him? 'Richard, my first love, how I long to hold your head against my breast as I did that time after George died.'

She was pleased to receive Sir Richard Ratcliffe two days later. There were tears in his eyes as he kissed her in greeting.

"There, there, lass, I'm not ashamed. We

all loved her and Dickon — God knows how he can bear this second blow.”

Janet curtseyed and withdrew as she perceived Sir Richard’s need to talk privately with her step-mother.

“I am waiting to leave for home. I am glad to have spoken with you first.”

“The King, has *he* spoken with you since —”

“No.”

Ratcliffe sighed heavily as he seated himself. “He goes through the motions of attending Council business. He talks to us. He’s alive and yet not alive. Part of him lies with her in the grave.”

“We must give him time. He will know soon that his duty to the Realm must —”

He interrupted her gruffly. “Aye, but we can grant him no time for — for what must be done.”

Her grey eyes met his troubled ones levelly.

He cleared his throat. “I’m a plain man, Catherine. I speak from the heart and devil take the consequences. You will remember I was in attendance on His Grace the night — before you left for Burgundy.”

She did not drop her gaze. “Yes?”

“The King has a deep regard for you. Do you love him still? I mean —”

“I know what you mean, Sir Richard. In

what way do you believe that I can serve His Grace?"

"There is talk about the Court, ugly, venomous gossip. You will have noted how fond he is of the Lady Bessy. At Christmas you saw —" He swallowed, rubbed the side of his nose reflectively. "It has been said he desired to wed her and worse, that he wished Anne dead, and brought her end sooner by poison."

Catherine made a little wounded cry, hastily stifled. Though she had feared — this last enormity! Was Richard to be spared nothing?

"He will send for you before you go, I am sure of it. He will thank you, speak of her, then — then you will have opportunity to make him see — he must deny this rumour. The men of the north would never stomach such a deadly insult to the memory of Warwick's daughter."

"Let me understand you. You wish me to convince him of the necessity of publicly denying this foul accusation? To do so is to admit the merest possibility of truth in its foundation."

"It is necessary," he said bleakly.

She recalled the urgency of the Queen's summons, her dying words, 'I think you are aware of the danger.' She felt herself tasting salt blood on her lip where she had bitten down on it savagely. Ratcliffe was watching her anxiously.

"He will trust your motives. Mine are suspect." She looked at him sharply and he blinked unhappily. "Catesby and I were instrumental in obtaining the death warrants of Earl Rivers, the Lady Elizabeth's uncle, and that of her half brother, Sir Richard Grey. It will appear that I, personally, have reasons to fear the lady's elevation, should she become Queen. I oversaw the executions at Pontefract."

She stood up, moving away from him, as if his nearness influenced her thinking.

"It will not be easy, Sir Richard. I will try."

He nodded, avoiding her gaze as she came back to her chair. Again the echo of Anne's voice intruded. 'They will trust you, yours is the old, Middleham allegiance, Ratcliffe, Lovell, Brackenbury —'

They went on to talk of other things, and, for once, she was relieved when he stood up to go. She could see he was still troubled. He hesitated, cleared his throat, a gesture habitual with him when embarrassed. "Catherine, so that you may see how urgent this business is, I will hold nothing back. The Lady Elizabeth wrote to My Lord of Norfolk."

"About the King?"

"She asked for his help in advancing her

cause, even suggesting a marriage if papal dispensation could be obtained."

Catherine gave a sudden intake of breath. "Then the King knows?"

"Norfolk withheld the letter, believing it to have been inspired by her lady mother."

"I heard of intrigues between the Dowager Queen and Henry Tudor."

Ratcliffe inclined his head sorrowfully. "I cannot be as sure as Norfolk is that this letter was not the sincere admission of the Lady Bessy's love for her uncle."

"But, incest?"

"Aye, and there is the matter of the bigamous marriage. It cannot be, Catherine. He must marry the Lady Bessy to one of his gentlemen and quickly."

She sat for hours after he had gone, her fingers clenched with strain, her head aching with conflicting thoughts. She recalled the hostility of the Lady Elizabeth that first time she had come upon Catherine and the King in close talk and there was the matter of the gown. Anne had known and cried out for her assistance. 'There are more ways of destroying a monarch than by intrigues or poison.'

Yet what could be done? If Richard's closest counsellors dared not approach him, how could she?

The summons came sooner now than she

wished. She had waited for an audience, leave to go from Court, though she dreaded to leave him. Now she would have done anything to put off this coming interview.

John of Gloucester came to her chamber. He was a handsome stripling, tall and fair, more resembling the King's brothers, Edward and George, than his smaller, dark sire, but his eyes were Richard's, grey-green, clouded now with sadness.

"His Grace requests that you wait on him, Lady Catherine."

His bow was sincerely courteous. There was no arrogance in his manner. "He regrets he has been remiss in sending for you, but trusts you will understand."

"Of course. How is he, sir?"

The boy hesitated, swallowed, then looked away. "He sends me from him when his grief is too hard to bear in company. He will put it aside now. He knows he must." He paused with his hand on the door of the King's chamber. "I do not think you need to fear he will break down, Lady Catherine. He is somewhat withdrawn, not truly himself. It may be he will dismiss you quickly. That implies no lack of regard."

She blinked back her own tears. "I understand, my lord."

Richard had his back to her and sat huddled

against the fire. A wine jug and goblet were close at hand, the jewels round the rim reflecting in the dark polished wood of the table. He sat forward, peering into the flames, a slight figure in the doublet of mourning velvet with its heavy furred sleeves. He stood as she entered, the firelight glimmering on the gold and enamel of his chain touching the white rose device as if with a glint of derision. She curtseyed low, then rose at his bidding and approached his chair.

The marks of suffering were plain enough, his features deadly pale, eyes deep-shadowed, his mouth, which always betrayed his innermost hurt and bitterness, held in tightly. She had expected this final grief to have aged him but he looked curiously young, vulnerable. She recalled the young duke in the market place at Tewkesbury, overseeing those executions his brother had commanded, controlled, holding himself in tight check lest he reveal to the world his pain and distaste for the proceedings.

"Forgive me. I should have sent for you before this, Catherine."

She was grateful he had not used the royal pronoun which would have deliberately placed himself beyond her reach, yet she dreaded the dire necessity of using their closeness to wound him further.

She said softly, "My dear lord, how can I find the words —"

"You do not have to, Catherine. I know you loved her and she did you. She spoke of you at the last." He reached out and drew towards him a small, wooden box carved and gilded, but worn as if with much handling. "She had one or two private pieces of jewellery which she asked that I give to you. I have put them in this box which went with her everywhere. I believe it contained some of her few treasures at Tewkesbury."

She had believed that she could keep her control. She could find no words to comfort him and his suffering was more than she could bear to watch. She found herself crying weakly. He took her into his arms, held her close till the familiar feel of the chain struck cold against her breast and she fought to regain mastery.

"I cannot — cannot —"

"I know."

"Richard, forgive me. I should have spared you this at least."

He drew her to a chair, smiling faintly. "Perhaps this is what I need most, the presence of someone who is *not* trying to bear up. I wept when they laid her in the vault. I thought then how far she was from Middleham and the boy. The place was so dark and shadowed. She should be near the sun and light and cold air of the Dales where her heart always was."

"She wished to be with you, my lord, that was where her heart was."

"Aye, she agreed to leave the boy for my sake, and never reproached me when he died. Duty is a stern taskmaster, Catherine, as you and I have found to our cost."

She gave a little hard gasp.

"I must return to mine, my lord, soon now, if you will release me, but first I must discharge a task which I find almost unbearable."

"Catherine?"

"My lord, do you value the loyalty of your men of the north as you do my love?"

"You know that I do."

"Then you must heed your advisers and publicly deny that you have any intention of marrying your niece, the Lady Elizabeth."

She thought never to experience the deadly force of his fury. His eyes blazed and his fingers bit cruelly into the soft flesh of her arms. His lips opened yet he could find no words to express his shock and horror. She fought to withdraw from his hold, fearing he might harm her in his first amazed reaction.

"Forgive me, dear lord forgive me, but it is whispered abroad that for the sake of the Lady Bessy you had murdered your queen.

They have not known how to tell you. I promised I would — Richard, try to understand,
try. You *had* to be told."

He released her abruptly. "Go," he said
thickly, "Go, before I forget you are a woman
and dear to me."

She fell back against the table not heeding
the pain as the sharp edge bruised her hip.

"Ratcliffe and Catesby are frantic. Lovell
fears to wound you and will not speak. Richard, my heart's love, though it breaks your
heart you must do what they ask of you with
courage and dignity."

"Sweet Jesus, you ask me to be dignified
in declaring that I am innocent of the murder
of my wife? Do they think me bereft of feeling?"

"It is because they know what you are that
they ask me to speak for them." She said the
words quietly, distinctly, finding the deter-
mination to stand her ground, more concerned
for his suffering than fearful of his anger. "Yet,
though they understand, they say it must be
done. So many times you have found the
strength to do what was needful. You told me
once you took strength from me. Take it now.
Do you think I would have spoken of this
to you, I above all your subjects, had I not
recognized the necessity? I think it was for
this that the Queen sent for me."

He had his back to her and she saw him tremble at the sound of Anne's name. Slowly he turned and it seemed he had aged in those moments twenty years. What grief had failed to do had finally been accomplished by the enormity of this nameless accusation.

"Catherine, you cannot believe this of me."

She shook her head silently and he came to her then and it was she who gathered him to her heart and stayed close while he wept the dreadful, unendurable sobbing of a man in torment. At last he said harshly, "She did not fear —"

"Only for you."

"This damnable war of insinuation, none of it possible to refute or destroy. Whatever I say I damn myself. Christ's wounds, that her memory should be defiled by this —" He gave a final shuddering breath. "You can tell Lord Lovell he may approach me on this 'so delicate' matter, Catherine. Assure him I will not strike him where he stands, as I so nearly did you." He bent and kissed her fingers. "By the Virgin, I'd as soon have you by my side in this coming conflict as any of them."

"Then it will come to it?"

"Assuredly," he stood up tiredly, "and I shall be glad of it. Face to face, axe against sword, that I *can* face, Catherine, on my own terms."

"Yet you will be mindful that England needs you, and in time — an heir." The last words were barely whispered but he had stern hold of himself now and he gave the ghost of a smile.

"That too — in time. And so, again, I must lose you."

"Yes, sire. I think you know that though I go, part of me will always be here."

"Yes, we have faced our own weaknesses and ruthlessly dealt with them, you and I." He sighed. "Had I been another Edward I would not have let you go to Kingsford, Catherine."

"But you are Richard, the King who commands my love and loyalty and so you will send me home because that, too, is necessary. My work is done."

"And mine must continue, though it tears me apart."

"Because it is for England."

"Perhaps." He half turned, his lip twisting in a bitter smile. "Think you England would not survive under another King, Catherine? Or do we tell ourselves what we wish to believe?"

It was the first time he had even so much as hinted at his reasons for ascending the throne and to it there was no reply. She curtseyed low again and finally withdrew, turning for one last sight of him. He stood near the oriel window, his face in profile, one hand ceaselessly twisting the ring on his finger.

Perron Chauvet escorted her north next day. Janet accepted the situation with resignation. In all events these recent grief-stricken days and the haunted oppressive atmosphere of the Court had lain heavy on the girl's spirits. She had grown to love the Queen even in so short a time and sorrowed sincerely. Silently she helped Maud and Catherine with final preparations, expressing pleasure when she discovered that Monsieur Chauvet was to accompany them.

It was a decided shock to Catherine when she stepped into the Palace Yard to see another richly caparisoned palfrey beside her own and Janet's. Perron Chauvet hastened to her side.

"The Lady Elizabeth rides with us. There may be some delay. The King's decision was sudden and the lady unprepared but she has packed necessities. The rest of the baggage can be dispatched later."

"She goes to one of the northern castles?"

"To Sheriff Hutton. The King considers a Court in mourning unfit place for his niece at this time."

Elizabeth, followed by her maid, emerged from the palace. A man hurried forward to hold her horse's head. She was warmly wrapped against the chill wind which had sprung up off the river. Catherine curtseyed. The former princess's features were half hidden by the veiling of her truncated hennin, but Catherine caught one glance levelled directly at her as she moved to mount. There was no mistaking it, it was one of pure hatred.

Nine

Kirtle bundled above her ankles, Catherine conferred with Janet, Margery and Dame Walters about the preserves and spices needed for the coming Winter. She swatted angrily at a buzzing blowfly which settled on the leaded pane behind her. It was hot. Outside in the grass she saw Martine catch at Wilfred's shirt and he wailed and pulled away from her. Janet looked up and smiled ruefully as Catherine rubbed an arm across her sweating brow. August and the scent of roses and columbine came from the pleasance but the kitchen was still redolent with the smell of roasting meat and spices. She longed to join Martine with her younger son on the grass, but for days she had put off these tasks and Margery had given dour hints of doubts concerning the state of the store cupboards and cellars if decisions were not made soon. When the hard fruit harvest was ready they must have the servants organized. Already the soft fruits were ripe for the heavy copper pans, raspberries and strawberries. Their scent reminded her too sharply, of a summer day at Middleham when a yeoman's wife had made Richard and Anne a present of flowers and strawberries because Gloucester particularly enjoyed the fruit. It had been such a day as this, the Lady Anne radiant, proud of her son on his first pony, and Catherine had learned the sharp thorns of love.

Her thoughts flew to her last interview with the King and the dull aching misery of the journey home which had followed it. The Lady Elizabeth had scarcely spoken to her, only when directly addressed, and then in words of chilling courtesy. At Stamford they had parted company; Perron Chauvet to escort the lady north, and Catherine and Janet with Rob and Maud for Kingsford. It had been balm to her sad heart to see the love in Hugh's eyes when he greeted her.

They had sat in the solar that evening while she had told him tearfully of the Queen's last hours. It had been harder still to touch on the ugly necessity which had forced her to divulge to the King what all but he seemed to know.

"It was as you said, Hugh. I believe he was so concerned for the Queen's health and his fears for the security of the Realm that he had not so much as considered what construction might be placed on his kindly shown affection for the Lady Elizabeth." Her voice trembled. "I thought he would strike me. I cannot but think that a public statement is unlikely to improve matters but Sir Richard Ratcliffe was most insistent that the men of the north would require it."

Hugh nodded soberly. "The true affection and loyalty for the King has its roots in the north. Nothing must turn that allegiance from him."

Later they heard from Ratcliffe how the King had called together the Mayor, chief dignitaries of the city, Lords and Commons and officers of the royal household into the great hall of the Knights of St. John in Clerkenwell. There he had sternly denied any vile rumour of his intended marriage with his niece, the Lady Elizabeth.

'He has also written to the mayor and aldermen of York, explaining how he has been forced into so shameful a declaration.' wrote Sir Richard, 'by vile insinuations issued by men so devious that it is at present almost impossible to bring the offenders to book. This has been hard indeed for the King to bear but now that his intentions in this matter have been made abundantly clear, he can come to no harm by any further talk of this affair.'

Catherine had not been able to bring herself to tell Hugh of Lady Bessy's indiscreet letter to the Duke of Norfolk. Had the former princess fallen deeply and sincerely in love with her uncle and was this the cause of her overt hostility to Catherine? If so, Catherine could find it in her heart to feel for the girl. Certainly the lady's behaviour on the journey north was understandable, for Richard must then have made it very plain to her his reasons for sending her from Court. Now it must seem that he was imprisoning her in that northern castle, for, clearly, he felt the necessity of removing the lady from the eyes of his household, in further separating her from her mother and sisters for a time, at least. Fortunately there would be other members of her family at Sheriff Hutton, young Edward of Warwick and the Earl of Lincoln, now created Lord Lieutenant of Ireland, a post which caused many to assume that by granting him an office traditionally assigned to the heir to the throne, Richard was now openly declaring his nephew as such, until he himself married again and gave the country the hope of an heir of his body. Catherine could not forbear a stab of pity for the Earl of Warwick, whose pitiful reliance on the advice and care of others, would always put him beyond the responsibilities of supreme power and, besides, his father, George of Clarence, had been found guilty of treason so that he and his heir lay still under attainder.

She had not been able to contain her tears when she displayed for Hugh the contents of the Queen's jewel box bequeathed to her. There was a delicately enamelled gold reliquary portraying the Queen's patron saint, containing a fragment of cloth, the whole on a long gold chain and a silver ring set with lapis, also a heavy gold brooch set with a pale sapphire and seed pearls which Catherine had seen many times ornamenting the Queen's hennin. They had all been dear to Anne and Catherine laid them lovingly once more into the jewel box to be worn on special occasions and treasured, as Anne had done, for all time.

She had settled thankfully into the routine of manor life spending enjoyable hours with Baby Wilfred and Janet, thankful for periodic shows of attention from young Richard, for now that Summer had fully come he and Tom were about their favourite sports whenever leisure allowed. Now, though, Hugh was becoming sterner with his son, demanding time for his studies and regular practice with the weapons of war. Frequently as she sat in solar or pleasance Catherine could hear the swing of the quintain on its support, Hugh's shouted instructions and the boy's breathless replies.

And throughout those months they waited anxiously for news of Henry Tudor's threatened invasion. Richard himself had left her in no doubt of its imminence and his own impatience to meet and face it.

Leicester was agog with unfounded rumours. The Earl of Richmond had offered for the hand of Sir Walter Herbert's sister. Hugh spoke of Sir Ralph Ashton's commission as vice-constable which had been recently renewed and the squadron of ships under Sir George Neville which had been fitted out for the very purpose of intercepting an invasion fleet from France. Sir Richard Ratcliffe wrote that the King had unaccountably turned to hawking and hunting in his restless search for something to occupy his mind and in part assuage his sorrow. While his scurriers were repeatedly sent to the four corners of the kingdom to smell out any scrap of information regarding the movements of his enemy, the King ensconced himself once more into the royal apartments at Nottingham Castle.

Margery recalled her abruptly to the present.

"So we continue with the raspberries tomorrow? I'll get the wenches to leave all ready overnight. We'll make an early start before it gets too hot." She broke off as there came a shout from the courtyard.

"Rob! Rob Wentworth, my lady —"

"That's Tom." Dame Walters half rose, alarmed, as her son skidded to a halt in the doorway and Catherine hastily gestured for him to enter.

The sun had already peppered his young face with freckles. His light blue eyes were wide with dismay and his sandy fair hair grimed with dust and shining with sweat.

"It's Master Richard," he panted, "Sir Hugh sent me for Rob and father. We need a bier."

Catherine caught at the table for support then she reached out and shook the boy.

"Tell me. What has happened? A bier — dear God."

"He fell from his pony, injured his shoulder and leg. Sir Hugh says —"

Rob had already presented himself with two of the grooms. The boy repeated his tale and Rob organized what was needed. He put out a hand to prevent the frantic Catherine from following.

"Stay here, mistress. You'll get in the men's way. Prepare a day bed in the hall. It might be difficult to get him up the stair." Having discovered from Tom where Sir Hugh was he shook his head at the boy too. "You stay here as well."

Margery hastened out with Dame Walters

to prepare a bed as Rob had asked. Catherine forced her trembling legs to carry her to the still-room for salves and ointments. Tom, at her bidding, followed unwillingly. She questioned him.

"I do not understand. Richard rides well. How did this happen?"

"Sir Hugh was instructing him in the use of shield and lance. He lost control and fell."

"Hard?" Catherine knew well that the skilful manipulation of a destrier by knee grip while both of the riders' hands were occupied required expert handling and she could not imagine why Hugh had attempted to teach so young a boy. Surely he had had the wisdom to instruct Richard on grass but why the need for a bier if the boy was not badly hurt? Her panic rose and she forced her attention to the task in hand, hurriedly putting bowl and towels into Tom's hand and making once more for the hall. Her face was chalk-white when she saw the ugly bruise which disfigured her son's temple. The boy lay, eyes closed, on the bier as the men carried him tenderly into the hall and, on Margery's instructions, placed him gently onto the prepared bed. Hugh's features were grim, and his voice harsher than usual as he tried to conceal his anxiety.

"The boy's taken a tumble, Catherine. He was on grass but hit his shoulder and side hard against the mounting block. He'll come round soon."

Ignoring him, Catherine sped to her son's side to bathe his face and try to discover the extent of his injuries. To her relief his eyes flickered open almost at once and he smiled up at her.

"*Mamon,* you look frightened. Please do not be angry with Roland. It was my fault I fell. He did not throw me."

"Lie still, Richard," she said quickly. "No, do not try to move," as he winced sharply in attempting to sit.

Experience had taught her in her work at Tewkesbury to ensure that the patient remained utterly still, particularly if there was a possibility of broken bones with the added danger of distortion. Hugh bent and ran a gentle hand down his son's side from shoulder to hip. There was no mistaking the agony that caused the boy. His face whitened though he gave no cry but Catherine saw him bite down hard on his nether lip. Hugh dismissed the servants, Dame Alice and Tom, leaving only Margery and Janet in the hall. He drew Catherine to the window oriel.

"I fear he has dislocated his shoulder. There may be damage to the hip and leg. He must be kept quiet while I send for a surgeon from Leicester."

"How could you be such a fool?" she raged at him, her fists pummelling hard at his leathern jerkin. "He's just a babe. What in God's name were you trying to prove?"

He caught at her shoulders and shook her, not brutally but hard enough to take effect.

"Take a hold upon yourself. The boy is conscious. There's no great harm done."

"How do you know? We have not yet undressed him. There may be bones splintered — the shoulder permanently affected."

"Catherine, cease frightening yourself. If you go on in this fashion you'll unman the boy."

"Aye," she blinked back tears of fury. "This is always the way with you men. Man he must be while he's yet a child. You *dared* to endanger my son!" She was struggling to free herself from his hold on her shoulders.

He read her meaning instantly and his brows drew together in black fury.

"While you castigate me the boy suffers. Let me send for a surgeon."

"No," she spat the words through gritted teeth. "I'll not have some unskilled butcher do him worse harm. I would to God Perron Chauvet was here — dear mother of Christ, what am I to do?"

The mention of Chauvet's name deepened the widening rift between them. Hugh released her so that she almost stumbled.

"Christ's wounds, must you always believe that Burgundian our saviour? I tell you, I shall order —"

"You will not." Her eyes had become hard grey stones flashing hate at him. "If that shoulder is set badly he will lose the skill of his warrior's hand. Is that what you want, a crippled son?"

His own anger died at her accusation. He gave ground, his dark eyes widening in bewildered unease.

"Catherine, I swear —"

"Waste no more time in swearing. Send Rob to Sheriff Hutton for Monsieur Chauvet," she said briskly. "I know what I am doing. Have I not seen, times enough, the harm poor treatment can do? Richard must be kept utterly still, splinted against movement until Rob returns, but dispatch him now, at once."

She moved from him to Richard's bedside, smiling to reassure him.

"My darling, Margery and *mamon* are going to cut away your clothing. We'll do it very gently, for you must keep still, then we will bathe you and make you comfortable and *mamon* will give you a draught to help you sleep."

He was very brave while they tended him, Janet waiting quietly with bowl and lotions for the bruising. Catherine fed him with broth, administered a soothing draught of poppy seed steeped in wine, then sat by him till his eyes became heavy, wearily drooped, and he slept.

Tiredly Catherine made her way above stairs to see that Martine and Luce had put Baby Wilfred to bed. Maud was waiting in her chamber.

"Come, mistress, you must get out of that gown, then eat something and rest yourself."

Catherine glanced down at her gown, splashed with water, sticky from sweat and dirtied from the dust-stained garments they had removed from Richard. Thankfully she allowed Maud to tend her. The woman ordered up hot water and prepared the wooden tub draped with sheets over a wooden frame Hugh had had made for their convenience in bathing. It was bliss to let the warm water wash over her and Maud washed, dried and brushed out her hair.

Now Richard was sleeping, her first panic over, she had time to consider how she had wounded Hugh. Would she ever learn not to twist the barb? She had raged at him for risking 'her' son, not 'his own', and he had known it.

There had been talk in the palace that the King had some slight deformity of the shoulder, sustained, perhaps, in a childhood accident of this type. If it were true she had not noted it, and he danced extremely well. She smiled to herself ruefully. His enemies knew, to their cost, that he showed no sign of handicap on horseback or hand-to-hand fighting on foot. Yet the fear gnawed at her peace. Her Richard must not be ill-formed as a result of this fall. She would not allow him to suffer permanent disability because the surgeon did not know his trade. And she trusted Perron Chauvet implicitly. The King had entrusted the care of the royal children to him. He had been present when she had lost her child. He had studied under the learned Saracen doctors. He would know what to do now for Richard. Stubbornly she clung to her desire for his presence, however Hugh resisted it in his jealous rage.

That was ridiculous. Chauvet had never given Hugh cause to doubt his intentions regarding her. Her face flamed and she averted it, guiltily, from Maud's eyes. Catherine knew, when she was honest with herself, that Perron Chauvet's concern for her went beyond the normal interest of a healer for patient or friend to friend. She recalled his words when he had come to her soon after Wilfred's birth.

"I had hoped to be with you —"

Yet he had risked himself to get Hugh out of London.

"I hope Rob will not risk his neck on this ride, Maud," she said. "It seems a foolish whim, but I feel instinctively that Richard will be tended more skilfully by Monsieur Chauvet than by anyone."

Maud bent to look down into Catherine's face, clearly astonished.

"Rob did not ride north, mistress."

"Did not?" Catherine stared back at her stupefied. Had Hugh defied her after all? She had not seen him since their hastily exchanged words. She had believed he had kept from her sight till her anger subsided.

"No, mistress. Sir Hugh himself rode out alone some hours ago. He told Rob he could make better speed to Sheriff Hutton unaccompanied."

Catherine's eyes closed in relief. So Hugh loved her enough to heed her anguish. Who but Hugh knew the way so well? And he was in a better position to demand good service on the road, yet she had not thought he would take such a step, and, suppose the King should decide that Hugh's unexpected arrival at the northern stronghold was an overt act of disobedience which threatened the security of the royal household there?

She forced herself to eat a little and, despite

protests from Margery and Janet and Dame Walters, insisted on sitting by Richard's bedside through the night.

Ten

Richard was fractious next morning, moved restlessly and only when he perceived that the slightest movement gave him pain could he be prevailed upon to lie quiet. Catherine hardly left his side other than to pay a brief visit to Wilfred. The baby was utterly content and both Martine and his wet nurse, Luce, entirely devoted to him, so, thankfully, she was able to leave him safely in their hands. Janet was anxious to help nurse Richard and Catherine persuaded her that keeping him still, amused and fed would be her best contribution.

She bathed his face and hands and laid cloths soaked in vinegar against his injured shoulder. He winced sharply and the whole of his right side burned with inflammation so that the cloth steamed but the treatment appeared to ease his pain and he was content to lie quiet as she insisted was a necessity.

"My darling, it is vital you stay still until

Monsieur Chauvet examines you."

"But Monsieur Chauvet is far away," he complained, his grey eyes following her beseechingly round the hall.

"Your father has gone to find him. He will come soon."

Richard sighed, "Why cannot Tom come? I shall miss the best fishing."

"Tom has work to do," she said a trifle sharply. She was aware that Tom's presence would increase Richard's restlessness. "Janet will read to you or play guessing games."

Richard eyed his half-sister in mock, male disgust. Recently, despite a strong affection between them, her newfound interest in Court and fashion, had caused more than a little friction to develop. His was a world of hawking, riding and fishing, one which had until recently been hers, too. Now their tastes lay in different directions.

She laughed now at his disapproval and settled to tease him into a more tractable frame of mind.

It was just before midday when Catherine was informed by her steward that men-at-arms from the north had arrived asking to see her. Foolishly, for one second, she had believed the Hugh had achieved a miracle and Perron Chauvet was immediately at her disposal. Her second thought pushed the idea aside and, leaving Richard, whose curiosity was instantly aroused, with Janet, she went to the solar, requesting that her visitors be brought to her there.

Both were soberly dressed in leather jerkins without distinguishing livery, one a tall man, not unattractive in a coarse fashion, except for a distinct cast in his left eye, the other older, burly-made though short of stature, with thinning grey hair.

The older man addressed her obsequiously while the other remained slightly behind in a subservient position though his bold eyes raked her, so that she flushed at his half-veiled insolence.

"Harry Bailey, Lady Catherine, riding from Sheriff Hutton in the service of the Lady Elizabeth. I have with me a companion, Arthur Trueman."

Now she recalled that the older man had been in the little group of servants who had ridden in the Lady Elizabeth's escort from London some weeks ago. She inclined her head.

"I hope all is well at Sheriff Hutton, sir. How can I be of assistance to you both?"

The man stepped forward and placed a cloth-wrapped bundle on the table at her side.

"The Lady Elizabeth feels that when you recently travelled north together, she was so overcome with grief at the Queen's death and her dismay at having once more to leave Court that she failed somewhat in her courtesy towards you, and more, that she did not express fittingly her gratitude for your devoted attention to her aunt, the Queen's Grace. She hopes that this gift will, in some part, make up for her omissions on that occasion."

Catherine was astounded and bewildered. She had slept fitfully, dozing and repeatedly waking to bend over her son's form to ensure he was not in bad pain and the arrival of these messengers from the Lady Bessy completely disarmed her. Her stiff fingers fumbled with the silken strings of the package. At last the contents glinted up at her in the sunlight, a gold embroidered girdle studded with seed-pearls and small blue stones. It was a lovely thing and obviously the result of hours of intricate labour.

"Please convey to your mistress my delight in her gift," she stammered, "I am quite overcome. The Lady Elizabeth must not feel in any way obligated to me. My work for the Queen, little as it was, was gladly done out of a deep love I had for Her Grace, and I can perfectly understand the Lady Elizabeth's unhappiness, however I noted no discourtesy on her part to me on any occasion. Will you refresh yourselves, sirs? My steward will attend to your needs. Please forgive me if I am somewhat remiss in my hospitality. My son lies injured yesterday and I am concerned for him."

The younger man bowed his acceptance of her courtesy.

"We ride south with further messages from the Lady Elizabeth to her Lady Mother and sisters. We thank you for your offer and would be grateful for a brief rest and food before we take to the road again."

They withdrew and she touched the shining gift, still bemused. Was she misjudging the Lady Bessy in believing that her expressions of good will and this rich gift somewhat less than sincere? Sighing she replaced the belt in its wrapping, laying it aside to be placed with her other treasures, then rose to return to her vigil by Richard.

She was half stupefied and exhausted the following evening when Margery came to her side and gestured that she wished to talk to her outside. Richard stirred, thrusting back the light coverlet with his uninjured arm. It had taken all their combined resources to keep him even moderately still but pain accomplished what she could not and when movement was excruciating he would fall back against the pillows, piteously appealing to her with his hurt eyes, huge now in violet-shadowed sockets. Had she been foolish to insist on Chauvet attending the boy? Had she heeded Hugh a surgeon from Leicester could have done his work by now and the agony of setting be behind Richard. Would this waiting prove to have been ill-judged? Reluctantly she followed her elderly attendant.

"What is it, Margery? Some crisis in kitchen or buttery? Cannot Dame Alice cope?"

"It's Mistress Janet. I want you to see her. She's very poorly."

Catherine blinked with surprise. Now she came to think of it she had not seen Janet to-day. Yesterday they had amused Richard together and Catherine had assumed the occupation tedious and that Janet had found entertainment more to her liking. She did not blame the girl. Sitting with a fractious child was not a pleasant task, especially for a fourteen-year-old.

Hastily she accompanied Margery to the chamber Janet had formerly shared with Cecily and where now she slept alone. Margery panted on the stair.

"She was very sick at midday. I judged it was the heat for Mistress Janet's no glutton, for all that she's a rare sweet tooth like young Master Richard, but she's no better now, in fact I'm getting alarmed. Her skin feels that dry and flushed. I'm thinking it's a Tertian Fever."

Catherine saw at once that Margery was right to be so concerned. The girl hardly knew her. She was twisting restlessly in the bed, her breathing appeared unaccountably fast, and there was a strange glazed appearance to her eyes.

Margery's sought hers worriedly.

"Am I to send a groom for a physician?"

"It is very late." Catherine frowned. "Give her a draught to purge her, Margery, and we must sweat this fever out of her. Send for the man in the morning, at first light. We'll strip her first and bathe her. That should reduce the fever."

Janet was miserably sick again and her eyes pleaded with Catherine like those of Richard's hound whelp. Now she knew them and muttered apologies.

Catherine gently wiped her face. "Do not give it a thought, child. Drink this. It should ease you."

"For me to be ill — now Richard needs you —" Janet caught at her belly and vomited once more. Afterwards, as she lay back her breathing was quickened to panting, hard and frightening.

Catherine hurriedly conferred with Margery.

"Janet needs us more at this moment than Richard. Send Martine or, better still, Maud, to be with the boy. He should sleep through the night."

"And so should you," Margery muttered dourly. "This will be the third night that you have not been between the sheets."

"That cannot be helped. Dear God," Catherine whispered, "that Hugh should be away now, and his daughter so ill. *I* sent him, the Virgin forgive me."

Margery caught the half-whispered words and shook her head. "You could not have known that this would occur. Mistress Janet was well enough when the master left."

Catherine's brows drew together in a perplexed frown. Janet had not so much as complained of a headache yesterday. How odd that this sickness had struck so suddenly and become so frighteningly severe, for it was clear to both women by the grey light of dawn that Janet was very ill indeed. She rambled in delirium and it was all they could do to keep her in the bed. No amount of sponging of the body seemed able to assuage the burning of the flesh and Catherine was relieved to hear a groom clatter out of the courtyard on his errand to the physician in Leicester's High Street for the man was occasionally summoned when any of the household ailed. She left Janet briefly to see that Dame Alice had had a quiet night with Richard and hurried back to her step-daughter.

"I think it wise if we keep others of the household away from this chamber," she said hurriedly to Margery, "for fear of contagion. I have not approached Richard too closely." She was near to breaking down now, since her fears for Janet's safety piled themselves upon her increasing anxiety both for her son and for Hugh's impulsive journey to the King's northern stronghold.

As the light strengthened in the little room, so, it seemed, did Janet's delirium. She cried out in horror as if monsters had invaded her chamber.

"Keep it away, please, Catherine. Do not let it hurt me. I meant no harm —"

Catherine wearily stooped to once more bathe the girl's heated brow.

"Janet, you are safe with us. No one is angry with you, no-one wishes to harm you."

Janet's terror diminished apparently and she fell to rambling incoherently but the alarming bouts of excited frenzy caused the two women grave concern. Catherine counted the seconds, minutes, for the time she could expect their groom to return with a physician. Throughout the night she had prayed to the Virgin and now it seemed her prayers were answered for shouts, galloping hoofs and jingle of harness told her assistance had arrived. Gathering her skirts high she sped down the stairs to the courtyard. Horses coming at that speed belonged to no physician. Hugh had returned and before she had any right to expect him. Scarce three days gone but there he was, saddlesore, steps a trifle unsteady, as he dismounted with Perron Chauvet at his side, and, behind them, a tall, angular figure she recognized, with a little sob of relief, as Master Fowler, son of the apothecary in the Chepe, in whose house she had found refuge after her horrifying experiences at the execution of Colyngbourne.

She flew into Hugh's arms, so that he half-stumbled, cramped and over-wearied as he was.

"Thank God and the Virgin. I could not hope you would be here so soon, to-night perhaps or tomorrow. It's Janet, she is dreadfully ill."

Perron Chauvet hastened to her side while Master Fowler lingered to unfasten their saddle-bags containing their instruments and medicants.

"Janet?" Hugh could not comprehend her incoherent explanation as she hurried them into the building.

"She became ill yesterday, was sick, Margery says, but her fever mounted and her breathing is bad. She did not complain yesterday and I was with the boy —" She gave a great gasping sob, "Hugh I'm afraid — I —"

Chauvet pushed past her to the bedside. Janet was raving again and Margery making vain attempts to keep her in the bed. Hugh halted in the doorway, gave place to the black-gowned apothecary, and caught Catherine's hand. In the uncertain light she saw he had gone deathly pale but he kept himself under control and made no foolish dash to his daughter's side, knowing well that his two companions could do more for her than he could even consider.

"I sent for a physician. Last night she was sick and hot but her condition worsened hourly." Catherine fought back her tears. "Hugh, what can it be? No-one else has sickened. She has not been about the manor farm land, at least I think not. I was so concerned with Richard. Since I knew, I have ordered all to stay clear."

"How is the boy?" He put one gentle hand against her lips. "Hush, my love. I cannot blame you for neglect. I know you love Janet well." His features were tight-drawn with exhaustion, and she stooped and kissed his hand calloused and sweaty from his hold on the reins.

"In pain but lying quiet. He is in no danger, praise the Virgin, but Janet —" she whispered hoarsely. "I feared you would not return before — before —"

Chauvet called softly from the bedside. "Madame Catherine?"

She hastened to his side.

"You say the demoiselle Jeannette took ill yesterday?"

"She was sick about noon."

Margery had laid back the coverlet so that the youthful apothecary could put his ear close to the girl's heart. He straightened and exchanged glances with Chauvet then gave a regretful shrug.

The blood drained from Catherine's lips. "She will recover? It is not the plague?"

"No, Madame Catherine," Chauvet said gently, "it is not the plague. Do you know if the demoiselle ate anything yesterday that others of the family did not?"

She looked from the bed back at him sharply. "No, at least I think not. You fear the meat was bad, but —"

"No, Madame Catherine. The demoiselle Jeanette has taken belladonna — what do you call the plant here in England? Look at her eyes? Can you doubt it?"

Catherine's legs almost buckled beneath her.

"Deadly nightshade?" she whispered through stiffened lips, while Hugh gave a great start of horror.

"I do not understand, Monsieur Chauvet, Janet is no foolish child. She is country-bred. She would never eat berries or leaves, make such a mistake."

Those green eyes of his glinted oddly. "I suggested no mistake, madame," he said very softly.

"Poisoned deliberately? Oh, no, I cannot believe it — and —" Catherine tried to marshal her wits desperately, "we none of us are affected. I —"

"Just so, *certainement*. This is why I ask what she has eaten, *mais*, no matter, the necessity, *maintenant*, is to treat the symptoms. The cause we must investigate. But, Madame Catherine, I beg you, be cautious."

"Will she live?" Hugh's voice was calm but without tone.

Chauvet echoed Master Fowler's shrug. "We can but hope — and pray. You have purged her?"

"Yes."

"And she has vomited freely?"

"Yes."

"It will depend on the dose." He broke off as Master Fowler summoned him imperatively. Janet thrashed impotently on the bed while Margery and the apothecary held her down.

Chauvet looked back at the stricken pair in the doorway.

"It is the action of the heart that concerns me. Leave the little demoiselle to us, please. We shall know very shortly. I will come to *le petit* Richard as soon as I can."

Hugh put a protective arm round Catherine's shoulders and led her down the stairs.

"If anyone can save her, he will. Come, my love, you are exhausted and beyond yourself with anxiety."

"And you, after this break-neck ride." Her voice broke. "Hugh, I am so sorry. Forgive me."

"For what? You were not to know that this would occur, and as I said, the saints in their wisdom have decreed that Chauvet and Fowler be here." He paused at the stair foot to bellow for a serving maid to bring food to the downstairs solar and insisted that Catherine join him there.

She made a half-hearted protest. "Hugh, I should be with her."

"Chauvet did not wish it. I trust the man."

She knew the words had been wrung from him and, with a little sob of compliance, gave way and went with him.

In the moments they were alone together she reached up and kissed him. "Thank you, for going yourself. I had not thought you could make such speed."

"I borrowed King's post horses at Newark both ways." He smiled grimly. "It occured to me that Richard could not object since my errand was on his behalf."

She looked away, ashamed of her outburst that had made him recall the boy's parentage. He swallowed ale and meat hurriedly but, though he coaxed her, she could eat nothing.

"I had no problems at Sheriff Hutton. Chauvet agreed immediately to accompany me and the fellow rides well. The apothecary had some difficulty keeping pace with us, but he, too, doesn't lack for stamina when the need is great."

He was talking fast and she knew it was to cover his desperate need to have tidings of Janet. His hand shook as he lifted his tankard so that the ale spilled. He cursed, laid it down, then rose.

"Let me see the lad."

Richard was awake and delighted to have his father home.

"They tell me Janet is ill," he said looking from one to the other of them uncertainly.

"Nothing to alarm you," Hugh said quietly. "Some stomach upset."

"I'll bet it was the marchpane," Richard grinned. "I told her she'd be punished. It was not for us and —"

"What marchpane?" Catherine demanded sharply.

"The sweetmeats the man brought for you." He looked at her puzzled. "The man who came from the north. He brought you some bauble, Janet said, and —"

He winced as Catherine caught at his arm, jarring his injured side. Hugh prevented her adroitly from further alarming the boy. He was obviously forcing his own tone to appear casual.

"The sweets? Did you take some too?"

"No." Richard shook his dark head emphatically. "Not because I was virtuous, well," he nodded grinning sheepishly, "that is what Janet called it. I didn't want sweet things. Janet brought the box to show me. It was pretty, she said, and she would beg it of you later for a trinket box."

"How — how much did Janet take, Richard? Did you see?"

"Two pieces, I think. She rearranged the others again." He eyed her guiltily, "Then Margery came and snatched back the box. She told us our conduct was disgraceful, thieving what was not ours."

Catherine closed her eyes in sick horror.

Two pieces! She could not but think that the marchpane had been poisoned. Sent to her — with the beautiful girdle. Were two pieces of sweetmeat, consumed as a childish prank, sufficient to kill her step-daughter?

Hugh supported her as he saw she was close to collapse. He forced a smile at Richard. "I shall be back with Monsieur Chauvet when he has finished treating your sister. I shall require you to be brave as befits a gentleman who aspires to knighthood."

Richard jerked his chin, unable to conceal completely his rising apprehension for the coming ordeal.

"I am no baby, my father."

"Of course not."

Hugh clattered down the stair with Catherine stumbling, her gown impeding her somewhat, in pursuit.

"Where can Margery have put it? If others have been tempted —"

"Tell me," he demanded tersely.

"Yesterday two men arrived from — from the Lady Elizabeth. They brought me a gift, an embroidered girdle. No mention was made of any sweetmeats."

"There was a written message?"

"No, at least I don't know. I greeted them perfunctorily. I was so concerned for Richard. Dear God, I should have taken greater care."

Her tears came readily now. "The older man said the gift was in consideration of my kindnesses to the Queen and —"

"And?"

"He said that the lady felt that she had been remiss in courtesy on the journey. You will recall —"

"Yes." He paced restlessly over the stone flags of the solar, his back to her, as he peered out over the courtyard and pleasance.

"Hugh, she could not hate me so that she would wish —" Catherine swallowed hard. "Sweetmeats? Dear wounds of Christ, did she strike at — the children?"

He turned and his tall form now blocked out the light from the window so that the room's shadows appeared to close in on them.

"Who suspects?"

"About Richard?" She shook her head. "No-one but Ratcliffe and possibly Lovell, also —"

"Also?"

"Anne herself. She suggested — that she knew, but the birth of the boy, that she could not know and she would not speak of it, even had she done so, to anyone."

"But her niece, the Lady Elizabeth."

"I cannot believe that."

He sighed heavily. "We cannot be sure that the belladonna was in the marchpane but it seems likely since Janet, alone, as far as we are aware, ate from the box. Our first concern is to ensure that the sweetmeats tempt no others."

He looked up and, turning, she saw Chauvet approach the doorway. He came in and she saw he was smiling. The sudden rush of relief caused her to sway so that she caught at the table for support.

"The demoiselle sleeps now. She has been very sick again. Now she must rest."

"Will she —"

"I believe she will recover, Madame Catherine. The heart beat is stronger now and steadier. We must pray to *le bon Dieu,* but I do not think she took enough of the poison to prove fatal."

Quietly Hugh told him what Richard had said. Chauvet excused himself and sank down wearily. His green eyes grew wary, perplexed.

"It is possible," he said slowly. "Master Fowler must be allowed to examine the box but —" he shrugged, "such an act would be unpardonable. I cannot believe that of the Madame Elizabeth. We spoke together of her regrets concerning the journey. I am sure that her feelings were, how do you say — genuine? She showed me the jewelled belt."

"You knew the messengers?"

He considered Catherine's question. "No.

Naturellement, not all the members of the household are known to me. I understood that Madame Elizabeth was to send gifts and messages to her mother but by whose hand, I know not."

They were interrupted by Rob who approached Hugh quietly and announced the arrival of the physician from Leicester. Hugh went personally to explain that the man's services were not required, as he respected and valued his advice. Catherine insisted that Perron Chauvet break his fast before attending Richard.

She also insisted on being present though Hugh's expression told plainly that he would have preferred to handle Richard for Chauvet alone. She was wise enough to leave matters to the men. Richard smiled bravely.

"I fell, Monsieur," he explained gamely. "I had not sufficient skill to manage Roland by knee pressure. Wasn't it stupid of me?"

Chauvet was never mocking with the child, "Such misfortunes plague the most competent of us at times, Monsieur Richard."

His examination was skilful but Catherine could see that it occasioned the boy much pain. He winced sharply but made no outcry.

"It is as I thought, dislocation of the right shoulder, but the hip is not injured. There is evidence of bruising and sprained muscle but there will be no distortion. Now, Monsieur Richard, if you will be very brave, we will put the shoulder back." Chauvet gestured hastily to Hugh who took the boy firmly by the shoulders. Catherine gave a little cry as the boy's face whitened and a slight moan escaped his tightly-held lips then he was eased back on the pillows and it was over. She hastened to him to bathe his brow and sweat-soaked fingers which had held tight to the bed supports.

"He may feel sick from the pain," Chauvet said smilingly as he rolled down his sleeves, "but that will soon pass. You are a promising chevalier, Monsieur Richard. You must sleep now." He turned to Catherine. "You have been administering poppy? *Bon*, he should be fishing again in a few days."

Master Fowler joined them all at supper and confirmed that the poison was indeed in the marchpane.

"Mistress Janet is much improved. Fortunately the sufferer soon recovers once the poison has worked itself out of the system. Frankly I am surprised she has not succumbed. There was, I judge, a fatal dose in each of the pieces. Apparently she ate only a portion of one, guiltily hid the rest, and, praise the Virgin, had no opportunity to take more."

Relieved and exhausted, Catherine gave instructions for hospitality to her guests and retired with Hugh. Despite her need for sleep it evaded her, though Hugh fell instantly asleep, a soldier's trick she knew well. Over and over again she went through her encounters with the Lady Elizabeth, then saw in her mind's eye the two messengers only recently gone from Kingsford. Why should Elizabeth seek her life, for the gift had surely been meant for her? Was the motive jealousy, spite, or more sinister still, and did it threaten not only her household at Kingsford but reach out towards the King himself?

Eleven

Catherine woke heavy-headed having fallen off to sleep very late. Hugh had already risen. Loth to set about the day's tasks she lay for a moment then Maud came to her side with her bedgown.

"No need for haste, mistress. All is well. Mistress Janet is much better, though monsieur says she must have bed rest to-day, she is so weak. Master Richard has eaten a hearty breakfast and Margery has allowed young Tom in to entertain him."

"The Virgin be praised," Catherine smiled as she put on the gown and allowed Maud to cozen her to eat. "There is still much to be done about the house. I cannot sit here idle for long."

"Dame Alice is already organizing the first salting of fish. Work has gone on in buttery and kitchen while you were occupied."

Catherine's wan face lit up with a smile of gratitude, "I have excellent helpers here,

Maud. I am blessed."

"That may be because you are not hard to serve, mistress."

"Has Sir Hugh eaten well? He *is* taking it easy this morning, isn't he? Three days' ride without break. That would have killed some men."

Maud seemed suddenly evasive, turning from her.

"Sir Hugh rode out early with Rob and Ralf Bradman."

Bradman was Hugh's captain, a grizzled veteran of Barnet, Tewkesbury and St Albans and Wakefield before that.

"I don't understand. Surely there is nothing pressing —" Catherine's voice trailed off as she saw the expression on Maud's face. "Tell me. Where have they gone?"

"After those murdering swine. Where else?"

Catherine made a little helpless attitude pushing aside her ale cup.

"Dear God in Heaven, when will this affair end? He was in no state to risk himself."

"Rob had some intimation of where they were bound."

"I understood, London."

"Ah, that's what they said to you."

Catherine caught at Maud's hand. "I must know everything, at once."

Maud hesitated. "The master said you were not to be alarmed."

"Rubbish! Am I not more alarmed at being kept in the dark?" Catherine's voice was unwontedly sharp and Maud eyed her in conciliatory fashion.

"Rob thought he knew the younger man, he with the cast."

"Of the Lady Elizabeth's household?"

"Be not so sure, mistress. Rob says it was yon knave who followed him to Sir Hugh's hide-out in the South Wark."

Catherine stared at her, thoughts racing.

"But he was not one who accompanied her north,"

"No, mistress. Rob is sure the man was in the household of Sir William Stanley."

Catherine blinked rapidly. It had been Lord Thomas who had questioned her concerning her visit to the city. The brothers, though unlike in appearance and manner, were close enough about their affairs. But why should either of the Stanleys concern themselves about her relationship with the King or even rivalry between herself and the Lady Elizabeth? Yet rumour had it that the Tudor saw opportunity for advancement in marriage with that lady and Henry Tudor was Lord Stanley's step-son.

Janet was sitting up and fully herself again

when Catherine went in to see her. She looked wan, her eyes huge in the small face but she was smiling.

"Monsieur Chauvet says I must have eaten something bad, not unlikely in this heat. I feel as weak as a kitten but no longer sick. Catherine, I am so sorry to have given you cause for alarm just now, when you are worried about Richard. How is he?"

Catherine seated herself on a stool near the bed, putting out a hand to feel Janet's forehead. Chauvet was wise not to have alarmed the girl by talk of deliberate poison. Janet, poor child, fortunately, did not know how close she had come to death.

"Much better. When I went in just now he and Tom were engaged in contriving fishing flies. He'll be up tomorrow."

"You look exhausted. Margery tells me father rode out early."

"Yes, off on some manor business." Catherine thought it sensible to keep the reason for Hugh's absence to herself for a while and gave a similar excuse to Chauvet and Fowler when she saw them later, in the hall.

They had hardly risen from dinner next day when a messenger was announced in search of Monsieur Chauvet. Catherine recognized the visitor when he was shown into the hall, as Sir John Trenchard, an officer of the King's household. He kissed her hand and accepted wine.

"Your man arrived at Nottingham giving word of your journey here, Chauvet. It's fortunate I knew where to find you."

"It has come, then, the summons?"

"Aye, my friend. The King may soon have need of your services."

Catherine watched while their guest was served refreshment.

"Will you stay over night, sir?"

"Thank you, no, Lady Catherine. If Monsieur Chauvet can be spared we should both ride out at once for Nottingham. The place is a command post, the King's apartments a battle tent, Commissioners of Array returning to report, scurriers arriving and being ushered into the King's chambers, even during the hours of night."

"We have heard that the French King has fitted out an invasion fleet at Harfleur, but that was in April. What has changed the situation so radically, Sir John?"

"Ah, you will not know. Richmond has landed at Milford Haven on the evening of August 7th with a fleet of fifteen ships commanded by Philippe de Shaunde, no regular French troops, the scum of French prisons, still, they'll fight well enough, though ill-disciplined."

Catherine's heart beat faster at this calamitous news and Hugh still from home!

"But the King is well prepared, Sir John. Surely the outcome cannot be in doubt."

Trenchard grinned. "Aye, our Dickon's a seasoned commander. He's taken adequate precautions. Norfolk guards the entrance to the capital from East Anglia and will join Richard immediately he is summoned here, in the Midlands. Lord Lovell has been for these last months strengthening the south coast defences. The Tower's safe under Brackenbury's charge and the north-east staunchly loyal, praise God."

"Richmond's commanders?"

"His uncle, Jasper of Pembroke, and the Earl of Oxford. The Tudor has had no personal experience of combat." Trenchard attacked a pasty with relish. "It's this Welsh Tudor myth of descent from the Great Cadwallader which could bring these wild Welsh lords to the defence of the Red Dragon standard." He guffawed as he washed down the meat with ale. "Most will take the tale with the basin of salt it deserves. Our King is as well descended from Cadwallader as the Tudor."

Chauvet was leaning back in his chair taking no part in this conversation concerning what was markedly English affairs. Casting him a swift, doubtful glance, Catherine wondered what kept the man at Richard's side, his loyalty to the Duchess Margaret, perhaps, or had he his own reasons?

Janet, allowed down to sit with them, though still wan, said frowning, "I do not understand how this man can hope for support. He has no claim to the English throne, surely?"

Trenchard leaned across the board to grin at her. "He's a Beaufort, descended from John of Gaunt, don't forget, a bastard line, but dubiously legitimized by King Richard II. He remains the one and only Lancastrian hope after young Edward of Lancaster was slain at Tewkesbury."

The room appeared suddenly chill to Catherine. As if it were yesterday she remembered standing in a silent crowd by the abbey as the covered bier on which lay the mangled remains of the young Prince was carried through the great west door. The words of Somerset spoken to the defeated Lancastrians who clustered under the gloomy pillars of the nave, she and her father among them, echoed in her brain.

"Those of you who live must decide your own allegiance. Young Henry Tudor is in exile. It may be, in time, he will revive the Lancastrian claim, though his birth is not such to warrant this."

In that hour she had looked on the young earl as a possible saviour for the House of Lancaster her father had given his life to support. Now he threatened all she held dear, Richard, the love of her young life, Hugh, loyal to York, and she dared not think how a Tudor victory might reach out to destroy all that the King had loved, young Richard, recovered, vibrant with eager life, upstairs with Tom Walters.

"And the Stanleys?" she asked quietly. "We cannot forget that Lady Stanley is Henry Tudor's mother."

"We cannot, Lady Catherine," Trenchard grunted. "If some of us had had our way that lady would even now be occupying rooms in the Tower with her husband to keep her company." He glanced round hurriedly as if fearful of being overheard. "Still, my lord has pledged his allegiance to the King and we must not doubt him. Most of this summer he's spent on his Cheshire estates. The King gave permission but insisted that his son, Lord Strange, remain at Court."

Catherine started, "As hostage? Then that effectively ties Stanley's hand."

"Aye, if he possesses normal family affection." He rose, nodding to Chauvet. "Our King's well placed to block any move the Tudor will make towards the capital. We'll wait to see what Rhys ap Thomas will do. He pledged himself that the Tudor will march into England over his body, so we can but hope he'll remain true to his oath."

When Perron Chauvet came to her to take his leave she caught at his elegant hanging sleeve.

"You will take care?"

His eyes danced and those mobile lips, so prone to mockery, twitched. "Ah, Madame Catherine, how sweet it is to hear you express such care for my person."

They were alone though Janet was likely to enter at any moment, having slipped up to her chamber for thread to continue her stitchery. This time Catherine gave no indication of annoyance for his forwardness.

"I was overjoyed that you came so promptly when needed."

"I am always at your service."

"You think the King will personally take the field?"

"If he thinks the road to London threatened, yes."

"He is still under the stress of grief."

"But a fine commander. Allay your fears."

She plucked nervously at the folds of her gown. "You will fight?"

"If His Grace has no other more pressing work for me, *oui*."

She looked up at those eyes of his, her own wide, puzzled.

"Why do you stay by him?"

There was a little pause before his reply. "Perhaps because I am aware, Madame Catherine, that in assisting the King, I am able to serve one other who is dear to me."

She reached up to put the tips of her fingers against his lips and he captured and kissed them.

"Monsieur, you must know —"

"Where is Hugh?"

The green eyes were cool now, challenging.

"He has gone with Rob after the Stanley men."

He nodded slowly, frowning a little.

"I wish him home soon to keep you safe and others of your household. I return your warning, Madame Catherine. Do you also take great care."

Janet had returned now and hurried forward to bid Chauvet farewell so Catherine was unable to reply but she knew his words were well received.

It was hard, after Chauvet and Trenchard had gone, to force her attention to the chatter of the children. Again preparations were afoot for war and, as in the October, Buckingham Rising, Hugh was from the manor. Would he and his escort be caught by either advancing army? What could be her excuse if a summons came from the King? That night in bed she broke into a cold sweat of terror.

The next three days crawled by without word from Hugh. A groom, dispatched to Leicester for repair of harness, came back with little information.

"They say as how the King be hunting at Beskwood, my lady. No-one in the town thinks there's going to be real fighting, not if the King's enjoying himself, like."

It was so unlike Richard as she remembered him. Often he had fretted against wasted hours in the chase. Now, perhaps, his restless impatience craved such active diversion.

In answer to her anxious prayers Hugh rode in on the evening of August 20th. He was grim-faced and tired but she glimpsed a light of triumph behind the eyes that told her his errand had not been in vain. She was forced to wait until Janet and Richard were abed before she could question him. Over supper the two had spoken of little but the urgent tidings Trenchard had brought.

When alone together, at last, the servants dismissed, he drew her hungrily into his arms, wincing sharply as the sharp points of the brooch she wore pressed into his chest. She drew back instantly.

"You're hurt, wounded."

"A scratch, bruises."

"You killed him?"

"Our friend with the cast in the eye, yes, I had no choice. He fought like a fiend of hell," Hugh smiled grimly, "not that I'd have spared him after so dastardly an attack on those I hold dear."

"He confessed that the Lady Elizabeth —"

He drew her to a chair in the oriel and sank stiffly onto a stool at her side.

"Rob is an excellent scout. We picked up the trail near Atherstone, stalked them until this side of Lichfield, then we fell on the two of them. The older man put up little resistance but the other —" he shrugged. "I tackled him, shouting to the others to stand off. He taunted me, asking if you or the children had suffered greatly."

"Then it was done deliberately." Her mouth felt very dry.

"Very deliberate. I should have been more temperate and taken him alive but my blood was hot to feel cold steel twist in him."

She averted her eyes, feeling a little sick at the unaccustomed fierceness of Hugh's tone. He continued.

"We flung him into a ditch after searching him for dispatches." He nodded as she looked at him anxiously. "Aye, he carried letters to the Tudor from several gentlemen, His Grace must know about. I ride to Nottingham tomorrow, love, at first light.”

“Stanley?” Her lips framed the name softly.

“Both are implicated beyond possibility or pardon. The older man, Bailey, told us he rode for Bray.”

“The Lady Margaret’s man?”

“Aye. He was riding to Lord Thomas at Lichfield but Will Stanley has already met Henry at Stafford. As we rode home we heard that Lord Thomas was evacuating Lichfield. It’s clear he intends to hold off from joining Henry’s army until success is assured.” Hugh’s teeth flashed mirthlessly. “A cautious man, Lord Thomas.”

“But Richard holds Lord Strange.”

“Oh?”

“Trenchard said that as Lord Thomas seemed bent on holding off, he’d regret his tardiness if his son were to suffer.”

“Then Richard knows, or suspects,” Hugh inclined his chin, satisfied, “but he’ll need proof and that I can furnish.”

“Hugh, to go to the King now is dangerous. You and Lord Thomas —”

“Aye, I’m aware of that.”

She clutched at his arm, “You *must* go? Cannot you send Rob?”

“This time I’ll be at the King’s side, Catherine, whatever the perils.”

"Then I go with you with Richard."

"What? Catherine —"

"He'll not believe ill of you on such an errand, nor will he deny us audience. He rides to war, Hugh. He has a father's right. He has never seen the boy." She waited, her hand tightening on his insistently. "Hugh?"

His dark eyes met hers directly but his expression was grave.

"This may settle the issue of the boy's bestowal."

"I could lose him? I know it, and I know too, that I could lose all of you. Chauvet says the King will fight. If he allows it, you will be with him?"

"Aye."

She pressed her lips to the hand she now saw to be bruised.

"Then I shall accept it without complaint. The older man, did you dispatch him too?"

"No. Bradman and Rob hold him under guard at the gatehouse. He goes with us tomorrow."

She sighed. "It might have been more merciful if he'd died with the other."

"Trueman?" Hugh gave that odd, yelping laugh, she had often known him give under stress. "Faith, that's an unfortunate name for the knave."

"Why — why should he seek my life, Hugh? *Did* the Lady Bessy send him?"

"That information I failed to get out of him. Bailey denies it and all knowledge of the proposed murder. He swears the lady gave the belt only into his charge and he knew nothing of the sweetmeats. We can only assume that the Stanleys struck at the King through you, possibly suspecting you were instrumental in his decision to publicly repudiate the possibility of an impending marriage."

"But why should they? Surely it was better for their purpose that Richard leave the way clear for Henry to ally himself with Elizabeth Woodville's daughter. They cannot hate me for that."

"They hate you because you are close to His Grace."

"Then they could suspect Richard —"

"There is no proof. The boy is mine, born in wedlock. He resembles me in colouring."

She shuddered. "You gave no hint that time — when I lost the child. You were then in the councils of Lord Thomas —"

He went a little white round the mouth.

"I was then a little mad, I'll not deny it, but never indiscreet."

"If he guessed?"

"The man has a tortuous mind. It is just possible."

"Yet the attack could merely have been a spite of the Lady Bessy's. She saw me with His Grace —"

"Aye." He rose and pulled her gently up to him. "If all goes as I plan, neither Lord Thomas nor Sir William will live long to threaten you or the boy, beloved."

A great shudder went through her. "The King is beset on all sides."

"But his old friends are loyal, Lovell, Ratcliffe, Rob Percy. Have courage, sweetheart. He lacks none of it."

"This last year has near destroyed him."

"Yet Richard Plantagenet has never been known to give way to despair, nor must we. Now, come to bed."

She lay wakeful long after Hugh slept. Her mind turned on the events of her last days at Court. It had been Lord Thomas whose interest had been aroused by her visit to Hugh in the city, Lord Thomas who had sent Trueman to follow them on their next visit. Did the man fear any disclosure Hugh might make to the King concerning his former alliance with Hastings?

Catherine had believed, though without proof, that it had been Stanley who had placed that indiscreet letter of Hugh's into Lord Lovell's hands. If the Lady Bessy had intended to kill her alone, who had dispatched that other messenger who lay in a unmarked grave on the manor land?

Twelve

As it happened it did not prove necessary for Hugh to ride to Nottingham. Despite his intentions to set off early he slept late and Catherine refused to allow Ralf Bradman to rouse him.

"I've the men-at-arms ready equipped, my lady. Sir Hugh gave orders for an early start."

"An hour or so late cannot affect our purpose. I must prepare the boy."

The veteran started visibly. "You go with us, Lady Catherine?"

"Yes. The prisoner, Bailey, he has been fed?"

"Aye, my lady."

"Good. I'll send for you when we are ready to depart." She broke off as Richard with Tom at his heels, skidded to a halt in the courtyard.

"*Mamon, mamon,* the King is riding this way. Last night he slept in Leicester. Tom saw him."

The steward's boy came shyly to her side.

"It's true, mistress. Father and I were in the town yesterday. The matter of a saddle for my birthday. We saw the King enter. He slept last night at the 'White Boar' near the High Street."

"An inn? Why not at the castle?" Surely the boy was bemused by the excitement.

"We don't know. Father says probably to be near his captains. There was some talk that the castle was not prepared for him."

Hugh bellowed from their bedchamber window, impatiently tying his shirt strings.

"The King, you say, in Leicester?"

"Aye, sir." Tom peered up at him. "Father and I have only just arrived home. We couldn't leave last night, the town was packed tight with soldiers and the gates kept secure."

"Send the boy into the hall, Catherine, and a wench with breakfast. Why wasn't I wakened?"

Ralf Bradman shrugged uncomfortably and Catherine dismissed him.

"Send Jem to us, Ralf, and Rob. Do not fear. I'll answer to Sir Hugh for my actions."

Hugh impatiently beckoned Tom to him and gulped meat and ale.

"Tell me all, boy."

"We saw him ride down the High Street, it was a brave, rare sight, the King in full armour and the pennons flying, the royal stan-

dard of England, the White Boar. The townsfolk cheered him. He looked pale and small
for a king. His visor was up. I saw his face."

Richard was wild with excitement.

"*Mamon,* you said he promised once to visit
us. Will he come now, do you think? Oh, I
wish I had been with you and seen him, just
once."

Jem came hurriedly up the length of the
hall.

"It's unlikely he'll visit Cadeby this time,
young master." He nodded grimly at Hugh.
"There's word that Richmond is at Tam-
worth, sir. The King aims to cut him off from
any attempt to strike for London down Watling Street."

"Had the King his commanders with him?"

"Aye, sir, the place was packed with archers, bowmen and pikemen. The Earl of
Norfolk was with him, his son, young Surrey,
Viscount Lovell, I saw, and Sir Richard
Ratcliffe. I heard that Sir Robert Brackenbury, the Constable of the Tower, had come
up by forced march from London. The King
was said to be waiting for the Earl of
Northumberland to join him. We were forced
to spend the night in the swine market. Fortunately it was not cold. Obtaining a lodging
or getting clear of the town proved impossible."

"Then the King is still in Leicester?"

"No, sir, he rode out this morning over the West Bridge of the Soar heading for the High Cross, at least, so it's said. He was making towards Watling Street by Kirby Mallory."

"You followed with the baggage train?"

"Yes, then made across country to report to you, knowing how anxious Alice would be. The boy was beside himself —"

"Yes, yes." Hugh stemmed the man's chatter. "Rob, send out two men to spy out the King's movements. I must know where he camps."

"Aye, sir."

"Are the men ready to march?"

"Yes. Ralf has left ten as garrison for the manor."

"Good. See to the conveyance of my armour and destrier."

"Sir."

Richard's eyes lit up with delight. "You will fight with the King? Cannot I go with you? Oh, I wish that I could." He turned to Catherine, *"Mamon —"*

In his wildest dreams he could not imagine that she would answer him as she did then.

"Put on your best clothes, Richard. Tell Margery you are to journey with us. Bring a warm cloak and a change of linen in case there is rain."

"Catherine, under these changed circumstances, should we not think again? You and the boy should remain here in safety."

"These changed circumstances make it even more imperative that we accompany you," she said levelly. "Hurry, boy."

Richard waited for no prompting but hared off to his chamber, calling for Martine and Margery, Tom in pursuit.

Hugh was hastily completing his meal after Catherine had assured him she had eaten earlier.

"Tell me more, man. The royal army, is it a mighty force?"

"Aye, sir. My heart swelled with pride. The King wore his crown gleaming on his helmet. They say he has put on so little weight that his armour is the same that he wore at Barnet. He was riding a white destrier. There were trumpets sounding as the Duke of Norfolk's men marched first, archers and cavalry, then the King himself riding with the Duke and the Earl of Northumberland."

"So the Northerners did join up with the main force?"

"Late last night, Sir Hugh. Then followed the knights and squires of the King's household and the baggage train and camp followers. Tom's eyes were dazzled by the heralds in their fine tabards."

"The King rides in splendid array to show his people he goes rightfully to defend his realm."

"Aye, sir. The townsmen stood gawking. But there can be no cause for concern. Gossip says the royal army far outnumbers that of the rebel, Tudor."

Hugh grunted. Catherine could not tear herself from the hall, so eager was she for each crumb of Jem's news. The King's army was indeed great but if the Stanleys proved false! Her vision blurred at the thought of it. Hugh rose, pushing aside his trencher.

"You are determined?"

"Yes."

"Then prepare yourself."

"I can go with you, sir?" Jem requested. "I'm anxious to strike a blow for the King."

"No, man. I trust you with the care of the manor."

Janet's light slippers sounded on the rushes. She wore her gown belted high and aproned as if she came from the still-room.

"Is it true what Richard says, that he rides with you to see the King?"

"Yes." Hugh took her chin in his hand. "I can trust you to stay till Catherine and the boy return, guard your brother?"

"Of course." Her slender form trembled but she did not weep nor did she question her father's intentions.

Hugh's scouts returned after midday but already the whole household knew of the dramatic nearness of the King's forces to their village.

"The King is camped on Harper's Hill, sir, on Redmore Plain the Duke of Norfolk's force, and, ringing the village of Sutton Cheyney, the Earl of Northumberland's men." Hugh's sergeant was breathless but triumphant.

"And Richmond?"

"When we last heard, moving down Watling Street from Atherstone. It's rumoured the Earl spent the night there at 'The Three Tuns'."

"The Stanley armies?"

"Sir William Stanley's force is drawn up north-west of Sutton, sir. We've no word yet of Lord Thomas."

"Were you challenged?"

"We wore no livery nor jacks, just moved among the men as village locals. There's tight security, but we had no trouble."

"Excellent. Eat, the pair of you. Arm yourselves but join the garrison here."

Both men showed keen disappointment. Clearly they were aching for action.

"We'd hoped to be with you, sir," the sergeant said.

Hugh hesitated, then shrugged. "Eat on the march, then. I'm ready to ride out immediately."

Richard glanced questioningly at the prisoner, arms pinioned, legs tied securely below his horse's belly, well guarded by two of Hugh's men-at-arms. As if he understood the gravity of the situation and their need for haste, the boy allowed Rob to lift him instantly into the saddle of his pony. Catherine caught her breath at the sight of him, so small and vulnerable in the midst of Hugh's force, most of them veterans of Barnet, Tewkesbury and the Scottish Border forays. Hugh himself was not yet attired in armour which was loaded in readiness for his need on a sumpter but he rode his destrier, a hugh, bay stallion, and was dressed for possible action in leather jack and salet like his men. He took her bridle rein to lead her forward and his grim expression was briefly illumined by a smile of encouragement.

It was a short ride to Sutton Cheyney. She could hardly believe her eyes at sight of the village transformed into an armed camp, noisy with the tramping of feet, the whinnying of horses and redolent with the stinks of cooking fires and roasting flesh. The men they passed appeared respectful, saluting Hugh, and in excellent humour. Catherine's eyes followed curiously the women of the baggage train, the ragtail of every army, clad in brightly-hued though tattered skirts, hair blowing free in the wind, their laughter raucous and hard. One woman approached her mount, hand on hip, and reached out to offer an apple to Richard who shied nervously back from her. The girl, for she could have been little more than fourteen, laughed uproariously. Already she was big with child. Dear God, what would be her fate if her man was slain? Briefly Catherine considered her own position and that of all at Kingsford if a like calamity struck down Hugh. Gently she reproved her son.

"Take the gift, Richard. Where are your manners? This lady is waiting for your thanks."

He took it gingerly, thanking her in a high, clear voice and she reached up to plant a smacking kiss on his cheek then they rode on.

Hugh left her for moments to visit Northumberland's headquarters, returned quickly and nodded as he swung into the saddle again.

"He passes us through his lines, sends a herald as escort. God knows if we'll be granted access to His Grace. We can but try."

They were fortunate to encounter Sir Richard Ratcliffe overseeing the positioning of his own troop. He hurried over at once to clasp

Hugh's arm in greeting. He glanced from Catherine to the boy and signalled for them to follow him. Rob Wentworth lifted down Richard, now very silent, overcome with the excitement of the moment, as Hugh assisted Catherine to dismount. Her heart thudded anxiously as they approached the King's tent instantly recognizable by its flying pennants, the royal standard with its leopards and lilies and Richard's own personal banner of the White Boar, floating free in the breeze.

Lord Lovell emerged. Sir Richard approached him and whispered urgently. Lord Lovell abruptly raised his head, and looked at her, startled. She put a protective arm round her son's shoulders.

"Wait here," the Lord Chamberlain said tersely.

Catherine stole a glance at her husband's features and saw large drops of sweat glisten on his forehead. He lifted a hand and impatiently wiped it. Then Lord Lovell was back and beckoning to them.

"His Grace will receive all three of you."

Richard hesitated, staring up at her, wide-eyed. *"Mamon —"* All this preparation and hubbub had passed over him, leaving him utterly bemused. He was excited and alarmed, both at the same time.

Gently she reassured him. "There is nothing to fear."

Hugh said crisply, "The King honours us, boy. Drop to one knee. Remember your lessons in courtesy and do not fear to answer if His Grace addresses you."

A squire held back the heavy tent-flap and they passed within, Lord Lovell waiting behind them in the entrance.

The King was clad in unfamiliar woollen hose and leathern jerkin but his enamelled gold chain proclaimed him sovereign.

Catherine briefly took in the equipment of the royal tent, folding stools and table spread with maps and documents, a book of hours in a worn leathern cover. Behind the seated King his armour glinted on its stand. She could see that the body squire had been at work oiling and polishing the helmet.

He stood up and dismissed both attendant and Lord Lovell with a movement of his hand.

"Catherine, Hugh." His eyes moved to the boy who, despite Hugh's instructions, stood staring up at him incredulously.

Catherine curtseyed. Hugh dropped to one knee whispering curtly, "Richard!"

The boy recalled his manners and knelt too but he was unaccustomed to the movement and almost stumbled.

The King's voice was low, a little harsh, which Catherine attributed to his emotional response at the sight of them.

"Please rise, Hugh. Seat your lady, my friend. Boy, stand near your mother."

"I hope Your Grace recognizes that I am indeed a friend," Hugh said, his dark eyes searching the King's face for sign of anger or approbation.

"Should I not, Hugh?"

"Your Grace will recall that recently I offered my services but was told to remain on my manor lands. I am aware that in the past I displeased Your Grace, but am anxious now to redeem myself."

There was a little silence. The King had resumed his seat. He looked from one to another of them and Catherine saw him smile, so that the sternness fled and he was again the young duke who had come to Tewkesbury with a dearly-loved wife.

"Had it occured to you that by remaining at Kingsford you were guarding what was most dear to me and, in that, your service is beyond price?"

Hugh caught his breath sharply then he bowed. "Forgive me for misunderstanding, sir. I am deeply honoured but beg that now I may have leave to defend your body by force of arms. My men are equipped ready and I leave a fair garrison to protect my wife and children."

Richard made no immediate reply. He turned his attention to the boy.

"So this is your son, Lady Catherine. I have been promising for some time to visit Kingsford so I might see him." He held out his hand.

"Will you come to me, boy?"

Young Richard went obediently and he drew him close to his knee, bending over the boy's dark head so that neither Catherine nor Hugh might read his expression.

"Dickon, do you know I fight a battle to-morrow?"

"Yes, sir. My father wishes to fight with you and all at home pray for you both."

Watching them closely Catherine thought the King's lips trembled slightly as he said, "If your mother were to be left — do you understand me — alone, will you promise to be obedient and dutiful always?"

"I am not a baby, sir. I should be lord of the manor but be guided by her in all things till I am grown."

"I see I need have no fears for her — or for you. Dickon, your mother was my ward and I have always held her in great affection. To me you are as — my son." The pause before the final words was deliberate. "Will you kiss me, Dickon?"

The boy nodded though Catherine knew he was reaching the stage where he disliked to be subjected to demonstrations of affection. The King held him briefly in a tight embrace. Catherine was aware of a trembling in Hugh's body and her hand stole out to take his. At last the King released the boy and signalled to Hugh.

"I am minded to grant your request. Will you quarter your men, Hugh? Dickon will wish to see our preparations. Return to my tent shortly."

Young Richard's eyes glowed.

"I wish I could stay for the morning."

"Do not wish for battle too soon, Dickon."

Catherine's heart was touched as she heard the old, familiar family name as Richard addressed his son. Hugh whispered in the boy's ear and he bowed with youthful, compelling dignity and then with a sudden return to child-like bashfulness pressed himself against Catherine's knee. She kissed him lightly on the forehead.

"Remember your oath to your sovereign," the King said smiling, "your care of your mother must always be your first duty."

Hugh said gravely, "I have information concerning enemy movements and alliances I rode here to put before Your Grace." He approached the table and placed down the crumpled and stained letters he had taken from the dead Stanley messenger, Trueman.

The King glanced at them hastily. "I have had some warning of this matter, but I thank you, Hugh. Is the courier taken?"

"One dead, one under armed escort for interrogation, though I fear he will divulge little more than I already know and can lay before your captains."

The King nodded. "Confer with Norfolk and Ratcliffe."

Hugh stooped and kissed the King's extended hand, rose and beckoned to the boy, then led him from the tent. Catherine was aware of his lingering expression of loving concern mingled with doubt. She sat, huddled on the stool, her eyes misted, dry-mouthed until she and the King were alone together.

Suddenly she was aware that he was very close and he bent and drew her into his arms. To-day she was determined not to break down and he held her at arm's length, at last, after kissing her brow gently.

"Thank you — for bringing the boy and yourself."

"You trust Hugh, will keep him by your side?"

"Catherine, I always have. I would I could leave him at Kingsford with you."

"It would break him to have no part in this."
He inclined his head.

She said huskily, "You are confident? Your army outnumbers this upstart Tudor —"

"War is a chancy business, Catherine, as you and I know well, but I am well prepared."

"You must not trust the Stanleys. Hugh —"

"I know. Lord Thomas, when summoned to the levies, sent word he was suffering from the sweating sickness. He also managed to contact young Strange who was caught attempting to escape my — protective custody. He was interrogated somewhat brutally, I fear. My friends were over zealous on my behalf. He betrayed his uncle, Sir William, and told us too of Sir John Savage's treason, but swore to his father's innocence. However —" he shrugged lightly, "I am grateful for this final evidence which Hugh provides. It is necessary for me to be very sure of — my friends."

"You trust Norfolk, Lovell, Ratcliffe, Rob Percy?"

"To the death, but Northumberland was tardy in joining me and I received a messenger from York while I hunted at Beskwood who brought word that the Earl had not issued the summons of array."

Catherine gave a great gasp of horror.

"I sent Spooner back with word to the

mayor and aldermen to assemble a force to march south immediately but the city is stricken with plague so it will, of necessity, be a small one."

"You will give battle to-morrow? Should you not wait?"

"Richmond is camped at Stapleton. I cannot allow him to move towards the capital."

"My lord, forgive me if I hurt you. The Lady Anne would counsel you to caution. There are those who would die to protect your person. Let them. Take no undue risks."

He was silent and she looked up into his stern face, fearful that she had angered him.

"The Lady Anne, were she here, would know that war is man's business and leave the decisions to me. She was Great Warwick's daughter."

"I am reproved."

"No, my Catherine." He reached up to touch the smooth band of her hair shining from the confinement of her hood and wimple. "Simply reminded that I am England's King and sworn to protect the Realm. Should I refrain from doing what I ask of others?" He impelled her gently back onto the stool. "Let us talk of the boy. He is all I expected. In case things should go badly — an advantage may very well be that I have never acknowledged him. I want you to promise me that you will allow no-one to use him, and I mean 'no-one', not even those who love me well — to his own danger and possible destruction. I know you are no fool and will heed me. How many know or suspect his parentage?"

"Your sister Margaret of Burgundy, Hugh. My maid Margery suspects and Ratcliffe. I think he spoke recently to Lord Lovell."

"Good, all these I can trust." Her lips trembled and he clasped her hands rubbing them for warmth. "You must not be afraid. We are all in God's hands."

"Are you?"

"Yes." He made a rueful grimace. "Any man who is not, before battle, is a fool, yet I am glad now of the opportunity to settle this — one way or another."

Despite her resolution she hid her face in her hands and gave way to sobs of panic. His lips touched her bent head fleetingly.

"God bless you. There have been times when I have wished I had heeded your pleas long ago not to wed you to Hugh Kingsford."

"I wed him of my own free will and I love him."

"You made that abundantly clear at Leicester that time. You were right. He is a fine man and I pray I send him back to you."

She caught at his hand to hold to her lips.

"I plan to hear High Mass at first light in

Sutton Church. My chaplains are craven and have deserted us, but one has come down from Bosworth to shrive us. It would please me, Catherine, to see you there."

She curtseyed low as voices outside told her the King's captains were anxious to report.

"I shall be there, sir."

She was woken before first light by the muffled sounds of men's voices and sat up to see Ralf Bradman arming Hugh. Outside she could hear the camp coming to life. Young Richard moved at her side, half roused, then slipped off again. She rose stiffly, fully dressed, putting aside the blanket. The tallow dips spluttered in the iron holders and light filtered in, grey and ghostly, through the flap of Hugh's tent. Horses snorted, harness jingled, men stamped their feet and cursed as their fingers struggled with refractory buckles on armour and leathern jacks. She went to Hugh's side to help fasten the buckles of his vambrace. He looked huge and unfamiliar in full armour. She realized she had never seen him so attired, not even for a joust. He stooped and took her kerchief when she wiped her fingers, greasy from the oil on the armour, and bade her tie it, like a favour, round his arm. Her fingers shook but she obeyed him.

"Thank you, Ralf. See the men are up and

ready to be shriven. Ask Rob to keep guard on the tent while we are at Mass."

"Aye, sir."

Hugh frowned as they both heard excited, raised voices outside.

"What's that, Ralf?"

"The commanders are grouped near the King's standard, sir."

"A herald arriving?"

"Not that I can see."

Hugh strode off to discover the cause of the disturbance. When he returned his expression was grim.

"What is it? The King —"

"No, His Grace is well enough. He's had a restless night, haven't we all? I'll warrant Richmond has slept ill."

"Tell me." She was insistent.

He shrugged, his brows meeting together in a black scowl. "Some further scurrilous pamphlet discovered by My Lord Norfolk pinned to his tent flap, a warning in doggerel verse, 'Jockey of Norfolk be not so bold for Dickon thy master is bought and sold.' Its sentiments are not new to us. The King will pay little heed to it."

"There is treachery within the camp."

His lip curled wryly. "True, we are not ill-prepared."

"Hugh, is there real doubt?"

"Aye, love, I'll not deceive you, if the Stanleys play him false. We depend, now, on the loyalty of Northumberland."

Both fell silent, knowing that the great Border lord had already shown himself tardy in coming to Richard's aid. The man was jealous, she thought, of Richard's devoted following in the north, where, previously, the Percys had always held sway. Could a show of spite now destroy the King's hope of victory and peace within the Realm at last?

She clung to Hugh. "My love, you will not throw your life away in some vain chivalrous gesture?"

He kissed her soundly. "I'll not court death deliberately. I've once recently felt his breath hot on my neck and I've too much to lose." His eyes went to young Richard still sleeping soundly, despite the noise outside. Last night they had discussed the need to send him back with Rob but he had pleaded to spend the night in Hugh's tent. Reluctantly Hugh had agreed. Rob would not move from their side and the lad was safe enough till the armies moved into the final battle positions. At last he said:

"Catherine, you are my heart's joy." He swallowed and pressed on thickly. "It has been hard at times to share your love but you have been a true and dutiful wife and —"

She stilled him, her finger on his lips. "I *love* you, Hugh. Believe that. Come home to us soon."

"There is a fair garrison but should the manor be sacked —" She caught her breath but he pressed on. "Ride with the children. Maud and Margery can be trusted to act sensibly, praise the Virgin."

She nodded.

"We'll leave the boy to sleep, Rob on guard. I'll not wake him."

He stooped and kissed Richard who stirred sleepily. Hugh wrapped the blanket firmly round his slender form as he straightened.

"Let us go to Sutton Church as the King requested, then you must ride instantly for home."

Catherine hardly felt the chill of the stone under her knees as she watched the King, kneeling unhelmed, at the altar of Sutton Cheyney Church. He knelt apart, the coloured glass lights touching his dark head from the window above. The familiar Latin fell on her ears, bringing a measure of peace to her soul. Hugh knelt at her side and she felt the cold steel of his vambrace strike through the thin stuff of her gown sleeve. A bird flew in and circled the small, hallowed place and fluttered out by the open door. The church was crowded and those outside knelt on grass and hard-packed earth to hear the words of the chaplain, hastily summoned from Bosworth. The King rose and moved to the door. The gentle clink of armour resounded in the confined space as his captains followed.

Hugh left her near the church porch. Ralf Bradman moved close in, in respectful guard position. She strained her eyes to where the King stood on a small tumulus near the roadfork to give his final battle orders. She turned, surprised, as her name was spoken softly in the well-known Gallic accent.

"Madame Catherine?"

"Monsieur Chauvet, I did not see you in the church."

He bowed gallantly and she knew he was thinking that her attention had been then for others.

"You attend the King, sir?"

"Yes, madame."

She moved some small distance from her watchful mentor. "God keep you."

"And you, madame. I trust you have a fair escort to Kingsford. Soldiers do not always attend to their duties at these times."

"I know so. My husband has provided a strong guard. The King requested that I attend the Mass."

"Ah." He was silent for a moment as his eyes followed hers to the little knot of attentive members of the royal household. "Keep the children safe, madame, while I strive to guard those you hold dear."

"Monsieur Chauvet," she whispered huskily, "tell me he goes to this trial with no innocent blood on his hands."

"I thought you trusted him."

"I do, but I would be convinced he is in a state of grace. I know my husband's heart."

"King Edward's sons are safe, madame."

"Thank you."

Hugh strode up, nodding acknowledgement to the Burgundian.

"The King intends to take possession of the ridge of Ambien. He'll be well protected by the swamp from Oxford's possible attack. I ride with the household knights. Norfolk is ready to move. He leads the van."

She sought to delay the moment of parting, her hand on his arm.

"Kiss the children for me."

"I will. All is — well?"

Hugh's expression darkened. "It is as we feared. The King sent for Lord Stanley's force, reminding the man that he held his son, Lord Strange, hostage. Lord Thomas sent back the insolent reply that he had 'other sons'. In his first fury Richard ordered the immediate execution of young Strange."

"Dear God."

"He has rescinded it. I think that wise, better far to wait till the outcome is determined."

"And merciful."

Hugh's dark eyes flickered. "Do not expect the King to remain unchanged by this. Already he has spoken to us with regret of the need to rule with a firmer hand from this day on. I think we shall see an end to his willing trust — and his mercy." He took both her hands in his. "It is time now for you to leave."

Chauvet moved from them as she lifted her face for Hugh's kiss. It was long and tender and she rejoiced that this time death came close to him he seemed unafraid. Battle held none of the terrors he had experienced in Warwick Castle. Then he withdrew to rejoin the royal household gathered near to the King.

Richard was taking leave of his commanders; Norfolk, Lovell, Surrey, Ratcliffe, Brackenbury, to each a handclasp. Last of all he came to Hugh. She was touched deeply. In all this company Hugh held no great office or boasted high rank.

The King turned and saw her. His gauntleted hand was raised in farewell. Her eyes lingered on the polished steel of his armour, as the sun's rays caught the gold of the crown encircling his helm. He seemed aglow against the light and she caught her breath at his warlike splendour. Did he not know that the crown could be his death, a mark for every arrow and axe-blow of his enemies? Yet she knew it was no arrogance which urged the wearing of it. It was a symbol of his kingship, round which those who loved and served him would gather.

She forced back her tears and raised her own hand in answering salute, tilting her chin that the two who loved her would see her smiling.

Thirteen

It was some time after noon that Catherine heard the sound of horses coming at speed and the hoarse shouts of men. She had spent the morning in the solar with Janet. Young Richard, with Tom, had obeyed Rob's instructions to stay close to the manor and had remained below in the courtyard. Janet had come from her chamber to greet Catherine on her return from the battlefield, her eyes red and swollen with weeping. She enfolded the girl in her arms, they had prayed together at Catherine's *prie-dieu* in her chamber, and then sat the long drawn-out waiting hours, Catherine watching Margery's foot on the cradle rocker, Dame Alice with her head bent industriously over her stitchery.

Now Janet sprang up to investigate, but Catherine cautioned her.

"Wait. That is no noise of men returning in triumph, joyfully. Rob Wentworth and the older men guard the gatehouse.

We shall soon know."

She rose calmly when Rob pushed open the solar door. She had heard him mount the stairs and his slow, heavy gait told her all she had dreaded.

"Sir William Stanley's men, by their livery, mistress, driving some of My Lord Norfolk's men before them. They went straight by us."

"Then the battle is over."

"Perhaps. It's an ill sign."

"Send the boys inside, Rob." Already she faced the possibility of a sack of the manor. So long ago, as a child of nine at Newburgh, she had learned to fear that.

She put a comforting arm round Janet's shoulders. "Take heart. We do not know the worst yet. If the King has felt a need to withdraw, your father may still be safe." Catching Margery's eye, she nodded.

"Prepare for a possible flight from the house. Try to keep the wenches calm. We'd best have bandages and salves in readiness and water heated."

"Aye, mistress." Margery lifted the baby from his cradle. He wailed fretfully and Alice hustled out after her. In the corridor Catherine heard Maud's voice. Thank the Virgin she had sensible women about her. She refused to countenance disaster, told herself she was making wise preparations, though her limbs felt unable to carry her and her tongue clove to the roof of her mouth so that she could not speak cheery words to the frightened Janet.

Her strained ears caught, at last, sounds of a new body of horsemen, two men or three, perhaps, riding desperately. Signing to Janet to stay inside, she sped down to the courtyard, as two elderly grooms ran to the horses' heads. Hugh, his armour dented and ominously stained, ordered them. His visor was raised and she saw his eyes smouldering dark against the chalk whiteness of his grim face.

"Henry Tudor is triumphant." He caught her close as she swayed dizzily. "Both Stanleys played the King false."

"Richard?"

"Slain, I believe, cut off by Sir William's men."

"Lord Lovell is losing blood fast." Chauvet's voice from behind reminded her of the need for instant action. "Will you receive him, madame?"

"Of course." She was incredulous that he should doubt her intention.

"It could be dangerous. With your permission we'll carry him to the hall. Are the trestles up?"

"Yes."

Chauvet signed to the grooms to assist the

wounded man. "I'll need hot water, towels, wine, salves."

"All laid ready against need."

"Assistance with his harness. It must be removed fast and hidden."

Catherine led the way, calling to the wenches for what was required. It was as if one part of her continued to function in this crisis, while her inner self retreated to some deep recess of the soul where it could not be hurt by the agony of Hugh's tidings. She thrust her grief aside while Chauvet needed her. Hugh moved off to the stables. Common sense told her the horses must be hidden, defences made.

Rob and Jem Walters had lifted the injured man onto the table and were pulling at the tightened buckles of his harness. She knelt to help them, straining at the stiff, blood-smeared leather straps of his greaves. He moaned and she saw that his face was badly bruised as his helm was removed. Chauvet grunted as his hand came wet from the back of his patient's head.

"He sustained a heavy blow from a mace or axe. There's some bleeding but that doesn't concern me for the moment. It's that fragment of broken pike-head which pierced his gorget. It shattered against the steel of the breastplate but the point embedded deep. I must probe and cleanse or the wound will fester. Pray *le bon Dieu* he remains semiconscious."

"God has not heard our prayers to-day." Francis Lovell spoke slowly through gritted teeth. "Get on with it, man, if you must, and hasten. I must get clear of the house. I endanger Lady Kingsford."

"Hush, sir." She bent to bathe his sweat-streaked face. "Do not torture yourself. We risk little by harbouring you since our allegiance is well known."

"God damn the Stanleys to Hell and Northumberland with them. Ah —" His curse was cut off sharply as Chauvet cut aside the leathern jack he wore beneath his breastplate. The blackened splinters of shattered pike-head were revealed. Chauvet gestured for towels to stem the first rush of blood as he pulled cautiously at the embedded blade.

"You are lucky, Monseigneur. A little lower and you would have joined your sovereign."

Catherine looked up to find Janet at her elbow, waiting ready with a bowl of steaming water. Chauvet smiled at her then gave his attention to the knives and instruments Rob Wentworth had withdrawn from Chauvet's leathern satchel and laid out ready for his use.

Catherine took Lord Lovell's hand in hers. His grip tightened painfully but other than one or two sharp gasps he made no outcry, though her anxious eyes caught the whitening of his lips and the thin stream of blood as his teeth bit down on the lower rather than give way to weakness. Chauvet rose after dressing and cleansing the wound and rinsed his hands in a fresh bowl Janet brought to him.

"Rest, my lord. Take some wine and garner your strength."

Hugh's voice came quiet from the doorway. "How is he, Monsieur Chauvet?"

"He'll do well enough if we can control the bleeding and pray the saints the wound does not fester, but he should not be moved for a while." This in a lower key.

Hugh nodded and moved to the Lord Chamberlain's side. The wine had done its work. Already colour tinged the ashen cheeks and his hands were less tightly clenched now that the agony of probing was over. It was clear that he was beginning to face the full understanding of the tragedy which had taken place on Redmore. He held out his hand blindly to Hugh and the other grasped it in comfort.

"I know he's dead, God rest his soul, Hugh. Can you tell me what happened at the end?"

"You know that Oxford's rebels attacked Norfolk's force on Ambien?"

"Aye, he held them and forced them back."

"But Oxford ordered them to stand firm by the standard and Norfolk fell. You know that the King summoned Northumberland then to advance?"

Lovell nodded impatiently. "I remember all that. Catesby and Ratcliffe counselled Richard to fly the field as Edward did at Doncaster. There would have been no dishonour in it. I would have added my plea to theirs but I saw his face and knew it would be useless. He called for his trusted scurrier. The fellow had a pair of eyes like a kestrel. I knew then he was searching out Richmond and the Red Dragon banner of Cadwallader."

"Aye, my lord. We all knew what His Grace intended and we understood the risks."

Lovell's mouth twisted in pain. "There must have been a hundred of us in that final charge downhill after the King, but I lost him, God forgive me, I cannot remember what followed."

"I was right behind you. I heard the King cry 'Treason' and saw White Surrey's mane and tail stream in the breeze. We rode right across Sir William Stanley's lines. I can see it now, red coats blood-like against the vivid green of the grass, like a picture in one of Master Caxton's books. The trumpeters sounded and we closed with the Tudor's men. I saw that giant, Cheyney, ride on the King, but he downed the fellow with one blow of his battle-axe and rode straight on for the dragon banner, his own standard-bearer striving to keep close to him. He must have cut down Brandon, Henry's standard-bearer, for I saw it fall. Then Sir William Stanley's men cut through our ranks. I saw you engage one of the mounted knights but he aimed a vicious blow at your helm and you reeled in the saddle. Your horse must have been hamstrung for it blundered against mine and I had all I could do to stay in the saddle. I caught your bridle rein and tried to pull you clear. It was a hell of stabbing pikes, swords and axes and the screams of injured men and horses. I could not see the King. You were unconscious and I fought our way clear of the throng to look for a refuge but a pikeman made straight at us and aimed for your gorget. I managed to cut him down with my axe but the pike-head shattered against your breastplate and I knew I had to get you out of it." He shrugged. "The King was surrounded by then. I guessed Lord Stanley's men had joined the rebels. I was dazed myself, I don't remember being injured but I've cuts and bad bruising, so I must have sustained them in that desperate ride. I can just remember reaching the woodland above Redmore, that's about all."

"I saw the King's death from where I was

at the top of Ambien," Chauvet said, his eyes on Catherine's stricken face. "His horse went down, but his standard bearer held the banner over him till the last. He faced them on foot. They ringed him round like a wounded boar."

Lovell made a sound, half gasp, half sob.

Catherine said quietly, "I think it happened as he wished it. He died England's King."

"He need not have died but for trusting too well in traitors." Lovell's tone was harsh.

"My lord," Chauvet said briskly, "you must make for Burgundy. The Duchess will receive you and there is need for you there."

"I'll not leave till I see where they've laid him." Hugh and Chauvet exchanged glances.

"The King would not wish you to risk yourself in vain gestures, my lord."

Catherine said shakily, "Did you see what was done with — with the King, Monsieur Chauvet?"

The Burgundian gave his habitual half-regretful shrug. "I busied myself with the wounded and they left me to it. I was too far away to see well. He was stripped of his armour. A horse was called for. It seems likely the corpse was thrown over that. Then I saw you, Sir Hugh, with Lord Lovell, and managed to assist you ride from the field."

"You are wise to counsel escape, Chauvet, but not yet. We can hide Lord Lovell in one of the cottages on the manor. Stanley's men will hunt for his body among the slain and when it is not found all routes to the coast will be watched."

"I'll not endanger Catherine," Lovell said obstinately. "The manor will be suspect. You should take her and the children and ride out now — fast. Leave me to my own devices."

Hugh signalled him to silence as Jem Walters entered and looked anxiously from one to the other of them.

"A messenger, Sir Hugh, from Lord Stanley."

For a moment no-one spoke or moved then Hugh said curtly, "I'll go out to him."

When he returned Catherine saw that his concern had changed to fury. Dull colour suffused his neck and face and he screwed the letter into a tight ball, after making ineffectual efforts to shred it.

"What is it, Hugh?" Catherine put out a hand to calm his mounting temper. "Is this an order for your arrest?"

"On the contrary, Lord Stanley writes to reassure me. He understands that I served the usurper, Richard Plantagenet, as he was then my King. The new King will not hold my allegiance against me. Stanley reminds me of our association in the past and says he will speak well of me to Richmond. By the wounds of Christ, I'll return him such an answer that will show that vile traitor my allegiance beyond possibility of doubt."

"And doom us all," Chauvet said quietly. "I beg you, Monsieur, not to be precipitate. There is more to consider than your honour. The late King would not wish you to endanger those he held dear. Lord Stanley's offer of friendship will give us time to secure the safety of Lord Lovell."

Catherine nodded, though she was herself, close to tears of mingled grief and fury. "Be guarded in your reply, Hugh. For all our sakes be circumspect." A gleam appeared in his eyes at the slight emphasis she gave to the word 'all'. He inclined his head slowly, as the sound of Richard's voice in the courtyard below reminded him of the boy's peril. He made a brief, incoherent gesture and left, presumably to frame his reply to Lord Stanley.

Rob, had left with Jem after assisting with the wounded man, now he returned. Catherine saw he wished to speak with her privately. She gathered her skirts and moved hastily with him to their end of the hall.

"The men outside wear the Stanley livery, mistress."

"I do not know yet if this is a trap but my Lord Thomas has sent friendly overtures to Sir Hugh."

Rob grunted. "Be easy, mistress. The man, Bailey, is dead."

She gave a quick gasp and he shook his head warningly. "The fellow could not be allowed to speak of what had passed between Sir Hugh and the King concerning those gentlemen listed in the dispatches the man carried."

"You were prepared for all eventualities, I see, Rob."

"Mistress, my concern was for you and the children, whatever happened on Ambien. Those were my orders. No-one is left to say aught of Sir Hugh's anxiety to report to the King and that first fellow who came to Cadeby, he lies snug enough. I'll see to it that Master Richard is kept from the sight of all callers."

She started, flushing under his regard, then touched his elbow fleetingly in gratitude.

"We must get Lord Lovell clear of the manor. We may receive more noble visitors." He grinned at the bitterness of her tone.

"Old Will Browne would receive him. He's grown querulous, of late, as you saw yourself last May, but he's staunchly loyal. His lordship will be safe there."

Hugh appeared at Rob's side.

"The sooner we get him there, the better, if monsieur approves." He had news for them. "Stanley's messenger told me the King's body is to be displayed publicly in one of the Leicester churches. He did not know which."

Catherine's fingers clenched convulsively on the table edge and he said quietly, "It is the usual practice. The people must see and accept that the King is dead."

"And — afterwards? Will they take him to London for burial?"

"It is unlikely, madame," Chauvet said. "They'll bundle him below ground fast and without ceremony. Do not let the thought disturb you. The King is at rest. He has naught to fear from his Maker. There will be time enough for you to hear Masses for his soul in Tewkesbury Abbey."

"Tewkesbury?" Hugh's tone was brusque. "We make for the coast and Burgundy with Lord Lovell."

"To fly before you are chased, Monsieur, is to invite pursuit. A visit to the Lady Cecily would not be deemed unnatural at such a time. She will wish to see her brothers and sister before taking the noviciate."

"And sanctuary is close," Catherine whispered, "but Monsieur Chauvet —"

"Hugh, if Stanley accepts your support you could be invaluable to our cause here in England."

"And live a traitor to Richard's memory," Hugh grated harshly.

"His remaining true friends will not believe

that of you. As for the others —" Lovell
shrugged expressively, "your sojourn in Warwick Castle and banishment to your estates
this last year may prove the means of saving
your life — and your lands."

Catherine's eyes closed involuntarily and
she sank onto a chair. Richard's words in his
battle tent. 'An advantage to the boy may well
be that I have never acknowledged him'. What
would be the fate now of young John of
Gloucester? Imprisonment? Could Henry
Tudor risk that rallying post for the remaining
Yorkists? Lincoln, Warwick? They would all
lie under suspicion. If Hugh were to fly now
with Richard, would the Lady Bessy's suspicions become fact? Richard resembled
Hugh. Should Lord Stanley remain firm in his
offer of support, they could remain quietly
here in Cadeby, Richard's future could be held
secure. Another sentence of the dead King's
flashed itself indelibly onto her mind. 'Promise
me you will allow no-one to use him, not even
those who love me well'. She had sworn.
Whatever anguish it cost, Richard's son must
be protected. Here, outwardly accepting the
Tudor's claim, she would die a little each day,
but what course was left to her? At the
Burgundian Court there would be constant intrigue, plots. Hugh would become involved.
She would lose him and his safety was very

dear to her. Her eyes met those of Perron Chauvet. She would fight with the tenacity of a tigress to defend Hugh and the children. Richard had known her inner strength. She'd not fail him now, though part of her heart would lie in that lonely grave with him.

"Your friends counsel well, Hugh. I have gone through this before. One suffers terribly but one survives."

He took her hands and kissed them. "I have said before, my wife, I can face anything if I have your love."

As he released her, one hand stole to her breast, where close to her heart, the little ivory boar she wore constantly was hidden. Both needed her. Richard needed her still. There would be time for tears and Masses but now there was work to do.

"Monsieur Chauvet, can my lord be moved now?"

"*Oui*, madame. He must."

Lovell allowed himself to be assisted from the table, painfully to descend the steps at the rear of the manor to the stables where Jem had arranged for a horse litter to convey him to Old Will's cottage.

As Hugh's arm lifted in salute Lovell said, "I'll ride into Leicester when I'm recovered, Hugh."

"I'll see to it, sir."

Catherine bent to assist Chauvet retrieve his instruments. The house seemed oddly quiet, as if the storms outside had passed over it and left it untouched. Janet had hastened to Margery to attend the children.

Hugh was closeted with Rob and Ralf concerning a suitable escort for their eventual journey to Tewkesbury.

"Monsieur Chauvet, you fear we would lead men's eyes to Burgundy?" she said evenly.

His green eyes widened and he smiled.

"There is Plantagenet blood in Lille."

"The boys? Edward's sons?"

"Richard of York. I carried messages to the Duchess soon after the coronation and Sir Edward Brampton conveyed the boy safely soon after."

"And Edward?"

"At Barnard."

"You have been tending him. Master Fowler's ride with you north —"

"He has suffered great pain, a diseased jaw, but I have been able to allay in some part the discomfort. He was unfit to travel and ails still. He seems content free of the Tower. He has a companion, a younger boy. The King gave instructions for any emergency — I pray he has been obeyed."

"You think the Tudor's agents —"

"Who knows, Madame? *le jeune* Edward will

need our prayers as will the Earls of Warwick and Lincoln."

He lifted a hand to touch her face as she whitened and stumbled. "The King was not mistaken in your worth, Madame Catherine. You will find the strength to endure. It is what all of us have loved in you."

Fourteen

Catherine shivered even under the heavy fur-trimmed cloak she wore. It was cold on this 2nd of February 1486, but she knew the chill in this chamber of Westminster Palace was due more to her concern for the interview ahead, than to the place itself, for the fire burned brightly enough. Young Richard was warming his hands at it and she saw his dark eyes taking in all aspects of the chamber, the rugs on the floor, the fine tapestries. Richard had not been to Court before to-day and was both excited and impressed. Hugh prowled restlessly from the window to the chair where she sat. The weather echoed their depression of spirit. It was raining heavily. They had walked through deep puddles crossing Palace Yard from the river landing-stage and it was dismal in the room, though still early after-noon and the candles not yet lighted. It had been anguish to come again, to face squarely the fact that she could not hope for sight of

Richard in corridor or hall. Henry of Richmond now wore his crown and had on the eighteenth day of January married Lady Elizabeth Plantagenet. It was the new Queen who had sent for Catherine, and caused her further disquiet by the particular request that Lady Kingsford's elder son should accompany his parents.

It had been an eventful and anxiety-ridden five months.

Their first concern had been for the safety of Lord Lovell, now declared an attainted rebel by the new King who had been hastily crowned with the golden circlet from Richard's helmet on the field of battle. Their fears were not allayed by the execution of Catesby in Leicester following. It was decided that the former Lord Chamberlain should accompany them on their visit to Cecily in the convent at Tewkesbury, dressed in the Kingsford livery as groom. As soon as Lord Francis was well enough recovered he insisted on entering Leicester, suitably drably attired, to see for himself the disposal of the late King's body. Hugh had gone with him. They reassured Catherine that the royal corpse had been reverently laid to rest in the Church of the Grey Friars but were unable to keep from her the snippets of gossip which reached her from the villagers.

Richard's body had been stripped, slung over his horse with a halter round his neck as a convicted felon, and carried so roughly into the town that his head had banged against the coping of the Soar Bridge, fulfilling some prophecy of an old woman who had seen him riding out proudly before the battle. As Hugh had surmised it had been displayed for several days before burial in the Collegiate Church of St Mary in the Newark.

In the privacy of her chamber she had broken down but the storm once over she determined to pledge herself to a renewal of strength for the bitter days ahead.

In Tewkesbury Abbey, Chauvet found her as she prayed near the tomb of George of Clarence.

She had not questioned his intentions, now he and Lord Lovell were to leave the Kingsford party. She imagined the two would make for Burgundy.

"I come to take my leave, Madame Catherine." He looked past her to the tomb.

"Can you believe me accursed, Monsieur Chauvet? The House of Plantagenet is doomed. When — when my father was executed, here in the market place, I cursed the three royal brothers, Edward, George, Richard, and they all lie in their graves before their alloted span. Now I fear for —" She shuddered.

"You wrong yourself, madame," he said gently. "What has happened is solely due to the hearts of men which dwell only on the aquisition of lands and power. You can have had no part in the destruction of these princes. Nor do I believe that God attends to curses, no matter how sincerely uttered in anguish." He drew her gently into the ambulatory where they could be unobserved.

"I, too, felt I had been gravely wronged in my youth. I will not tell you the details, they do not concern you, but I became bitter. I left my father's house determined to put first ambition and my own self aggrandizement. I travelled. I served many masters, performing tasks for some I would not wish to recount to you. I learned much of the art of healing which fascinated me only because it gave me some sense of satisfaction and power over others. I came to England in the service of the Duchess Margaret. I met a woman who needed my skill. From her I discovered that courage, loyalty, inner strength, revealed the true face of love, and have from that time ceased to be my own man."

Catherine swallowed hard. "Monsieur, you must not speak of this. You give me pain, and more I cannot bear."

"I know that you loved the King and that your husband is very dear to you. I speak only to assure you that your continuing welfare is what makes life precious for me. I ask for nothing, only that you recognize the gift you have given to me and hold it for your comfort." He had stooped and kissed her hands and that day had ridden from Tewkesbury with Francis Lovell.

No attempt was made to arrest Hugh on his return to Kingsford. Eventually he was summoned to London to attend before the King's councillors in the Star Chamber. He told her little of his experiences other than that Lord Stanley had given the support he had promised and, on sworn allegiance to the new King and payment of a heavy fine, he was able to retain his manors of Kingsford and Newburgh. She knew what it had cost him to accept ignominious alliance with the two Stanley brothers, now rewarded by the man they had helped to place upon the throne, Lord Thomas had become the Earl of Derby on October 27th, on the same day that the King's uncle, Jasper of Pembroke, was created Duke of Bedford. Sir William had been appointed Lord Chamberlain.

Throughout the bitter days which followed Henry Tudor's coronation they had comforted themselves with the conviction that their actions safeguarded Richard's son, and would have been in obedience to his wishes.

Now, suddenly, the new Queen had summoned her to London and all Catherine's fears were renewed and sharpened.

An attendant appeared from the Queen's chamber.

"Her Grace will receive you now, Lady Kingsford."

Catherine's eyes appealed mutely to Hugh. He inclined his chin, putting an arm round Richard.

"We will await you here."

They had decided on their policy. This summons could not be ignored. Please God, afterwards, if there was the slightest hint of peril to the boy, they would have time to accomplish his escape from the country. At 'The Crossed Keys', in the Chepe, Rob and Maud waited, all preparations made for instant departure.

Catherine sank into a deep curtsey. The Queen's voice was gracious.

"Please rise, Lady Kingsford. I regret I kept you waiting. The King's mother, Lady Margaret, called on me, an urgent, domestic matter." She signalled to her two ladies, both strangers to Catherine, to leave them. "Please sit by me."

The new Queen was splendidly dressed in a gown of cloth of gold over purple velvet, which, despite its richness, appeared strangely sombre. The hennin was of black velvet and the fur trimmings on hem and sleeves of sable. Catherine detected signs of tension in the lovely features, the mouth held in, lower lip drooping slightly, frown lines on the high, fine forehead. She held out her hand smiling. As with all the Plantagenets it seemed that the bright sun appeared from the clouds.

"It is good to see you again, Catherine. I wished to explain that His Grace felt it not appropriate that you should attend me as one of my ladies."

Catherine was startled. It had not occurred to her to expect such an honour, and her encounters with the Lady Bessy in the past had not always been congenial. She seated herself, as requested, on a stool near the Queen's chair.

"I thank Your Grace for your kindly intentions but I am happier with the children living quietly at Cadeby."

"Your children?" The Queen's very blue eyes widened with eagerness. "You brought your elder son?"

Catherine controlled the tremble in her voice.

"I have, Your Grace. He is in the antechamber with my husband."

"Please present him. He will be eight, will he not? You spoke so much of the children. I would wish to see him."

Catherine moved to the door and beckoned her son forward. Hugh's eyes narrowed but he gave the boy a slight push.

"The Queen honours you, Richard," she said quietly. "Make your obeisance."

Gracefully he dropped to one knee. The Queen ordered him to approach her chair and Catherine saw her eyes appraise the boy shrewdly.

"Your mother and I were companions here last year. I have heard much of you, young master."

"Your Grace is kind."

"You have not been to Court?"

"No, Your Grace."

"You'll soon be of an age to serve as page and squire. Would you like to enter my household, Richard?"

Catherine's lips parted in a little gasp. In the light from the oriel he looked so slight and vulnerable. Did the Queen note those resemblances she knew so well, the frown of concentration which formed now as he considered the Queen's words, the slight ironic twist to the lips which pronounced him Richard's son, or were they apparent only to her, who had so deeply loved his father? In all else he resembled Hugh, save he would not grow so tall.

The boy's eyes sparkled. "I would indeed,

Your Grace, if my father approves."

"We must seek his consent. Your manners are excellent. I am sure I could rely on you for good service." The Queen extended her hand for the boy to kiss. "Leave me now with your mother, Dickon."

Again Catherine's heart leaped. Had the nickname been used deliberately? Richard peered into her face for signs of her approval. She reassured him.

"The Queen is pleased, Richard, I will join you soon."

The door closed on him and the Queen let out a little sigh.

"I had to see him first. He resembles your husband. That is good."

"Your Grace —" Catherine's voice was husky, her mouth dry with apprehension.

"Catherine, I will not ask — anything, but I cannot fail to guess. We both had great — affection for my late uncle." There was a slight pause before the word, the tone scarce whispered. "You must see that for the boy to enter my household would be his greatest safeguard."

"But —"

"Under the King's eye, to what harm could he come, and I swear I will protect him with all the skills of mind and body? I have become adept at sharpening them all."

The two women eyed each other and the Queen reached for and took Catherine's hand.

"We will be grateful for the appointment," Catherine answered mechanically.

"They will all be in peril, John of Lincoln, John of Gloucester, Young Warwick. There must be no possibility of secret visitors to Cadeby in touch with Hugh or the boy. Trust me, Catherine. Believe that I wish you well."

"I cannot think — I was grateful for the marks of favour. The belt you sent me. I wore it to-day," Catherine touched the soft leather fleetingly, "and the sweetmeats for the children."

"Sweetmeats?" The Queen looked puzzled. "I sent none, but perhaps some member of the household thought they would be appreciated." She gave a little laugh. "My mother, always vain for our looks and mindful of spoiling our teeth, would never allow Cecily or I to eat them, and, fortunately, I have not acquired a weakness. I am glad they were well received."

The flood of relief which swept through Catherine threatened to unbalance her and she was glad to resume her stool. The Queen leaned forward urgently.

"You have seen where they have laid him?"

"Yes, Your Grace, it is secluded, safe from the noise and bustle of Leicester town."

"Thank you." Her fingers gripped Catherine's arm. "Hugh will be circumspect as all of us must?"

"Yes, Your Grace."

"Then God give you peace at Cadeby. I will send for the boy when the time is right."

Catherine rose and curtseyed. Again their eyes met. The Queen's guard was lowered momentarily and Catherine was able to glimpse a measure of her suffering. She had achieved what had been the summit of her mother's ambition for her. She wore the Crown of England, though Henry had not yet shown signs of allowing her official anointing and coronation, for which all England waited, yet Catherine's woman's heart went out to her in pity. At what a cost did this woman unite the warring factions of Lancastrians and Yorkists? Catherine had herself performed a like service for her own retainers by her marriage with Hugh.

"I wish you all the peace and happiness my marriage has brought to me, Your Grace," she said humbly.

"You love Hugh dearly?"

"Yes."

"I am glad of it. Be of good heart concerning your son's safety."

They clasped hands briefly. So little had been said, so much understood. Catherine curtseyed and withdrew.

Outside Hugh and her son awaited her.

She held Richard tight-pressed to her heart. Hugh's dark eyes glimmered with the faintest hint of tears. She was overcome with her love for him, and remorse for the anguish she had often cost him.

"We can go home now," she said softly. "I believe all will be well with us."

The employees of THORNDIKE PRESS hope you have enjoyed this Large Print book. All our Large Print books are designed for easy reading — and they're made to last.

Other Thorndike Large Print books are available at your library, through selected bookstores, or directly from us. Suggestions for books you would like to see in Large Print are always welcome.

For more information about current and upcoming titles, please call or mail your name and address to:

THORNDIKE PRESS
PO Box 159
Thorndike, Maine 04986
800/223-6121
207/948-2962